I0545288

The Start

A Rebellion LIT Anthology

Rebellion LIT

Cover Design by Tiffany Christina Lewis
Title Card Illustrations by Victoria Aden

ASTRID
by Ria Hill

Astrid

By Ria Hill

Another morning after.

It happens every so often. I go to sleep one night, they make me go to sleep that night, and I wake up sore. And naked, and dirty with blood.

Not my blood, though. Somebody else's blood.

It does not hurt, when they make me go to sleep. Not a lot anyway. Just a little prick.

They say that it is for my own good and the next thing I know, the room is floating and then it is morning, and light is streaming into my bedroom and I am sore. And naked, and dirty with blood. Blood that is not mine. I have asked them before, to not make me go to sleep. But they said I could not make that choice. Not yet.

I ask them when, and they say when I am old enough. I think they think I will forget and just keep letting them do it. But every time they do it, I make a mark. They told me they do it twelve times a year only. Maybe a little more. They told me that when it has been five years, I will be old enough.

Today will be the sixty-third time they are going to make me sleep, and I cannot wait any longer. I have to ask today.

"Doctor Brown," I say. He is setting things up to make me go to sleep, but I will not let him this time. "Am I older yet?"

He stops moving and looks at me. He is not an old man, but he is gray above his ears. His hair, though lightening, is still thick and strong. Glasses, framed with wire, balance low on his nose. His mouth is a line of displeasure.

"Astrid," he says. "We've been over this."

"We were over this sixty times ago," I insist. "Please, Doctor Brown. Let me stay awake."

Doctor Brown looks around. He looks back at me. He sighs through his nose in a big hurrumph.

"Okay," he says. He takes the shot and puts it away. "But you have to pretend to be asleep until you can't anymore. Do you understand?"

I do not understand, but I nod anyway. I want to know what I miss every time they make me go to sleep.

"Hop up, kiddo," he says. I climb on the cot with the wheels and pretend to be asleep.

The doctor knocks on the door of my room, always locked, and says, "She's out."

There is a *buzz buzz* as the door unlocks, and then

there are other feet in the room. Other shoes than Doctor Brown's. My cot wheels are unlocked, and we start to roll out of my room.

It is hard to pretend to be asleep when I have only been outside my room a very few times in my life. Well, maybe not in my life, but since I was very small. When I turned old enough for blood to come out of me between my legs, they put me in my room and there I have stayed.

I like my room, but outside must be so large to have as many people in it as I can hear now.

"What's on the menu tonight?" one strange voice says.

"Well, the bitch is pretty well full grown," a man answers. He has a funny accent, like on the Monty Python show they let me watch sometimes. "We thought we'd try something a little different."

"You don't mean..." That one is Doctor Brown.

"About bloody time, don't you think?" says the funny accent. "It's why she's here, after all."

I can hear Doctor Brown breathing hard, like real close. I can picture his mouth, a line of worrying.

"Maybe one more month," he says. "Next cycle she should be—"

"Or now." Funny accent sounds bored. "Everything is all set up, unless you're squeamish."

I do not know that word, but we are here. The wheels get locked down again and everybody walks away. Buzz buzz the door goes locked. And I am alone again.

Can I open my eyes now? Is this when Doctor

Brown meant? I decide to take a small peek. Really small, so no one can see. My head is lying on its side already, so I open my eyes just a sliver without moving.

I see a big shiny window, and all the men in lab coats like Doctor Brown are watching me. I also see there is another man in the room with me, but he is asleep for real, on the floor.

I guess they were not quite as careful with him as they were with me. His arm is up, and I am not sure why until I see there is a little string holding his wrist to a hook on the wall. He moves pretty soon.

It looks like it hurts his head to move, but then he sits up. He tries to pull his hand off the wall, but the string must be really very strong or else he would be able to break it. He looks pretty strong, too.

"You fuckers," he says. "You fuckers!" His voice is so loud I jump. Then he sees me. I give up and open my eyes.

The men in the lab coats are all buzz buzzing around, but they aren't opening the door.

Someone is yelling at Doctor Brown, but I can't hear what he is saying. "Hey, little girl," says the man on the floor.

"I am not little," I say. "I am seventeen, I think."

They said I was twelve when I started to bleed. I heard them. I am very probably seventeen.

"Do you wanna do me a solid and find something to cut me loose?" he says.

"Do you a solid?" I repeat.

I do not know what that means. I sit up finally and

look around. There is a big window on the wall away from the glass. The doctors are all buzz buzzing behind. I can see a little light coming through, but there's a curtain there.

"Yeah," he says. "Like, help me out." Suddenly, there is a crack crackle and the speakers on the walls pop loud.

"Astrid," says the voice. It is Doctor Brown. He sounds sad. "I need you to listen to me. That man is very dangerous, do you understand? You need to stay where you are."

I look back at the man against the wall and stare at him for a minute. He doesn't look very dangerous. He looks mad, but not like he wants to hurt me. More like he wants to hurt Doctor Brown and the other doctors.

"Do you understand?"

"Yeah, I understand!" I say it real loud so I know he can hear me even on the other side of the glass.

"Good girl," he says. Then there is a shuffle and the man who was yelling at Doctor Brown starts to talk. He's the man with the funny accent like Monty Python.

"Clark," he says. The man on the floor's head snaps up to listen. His name must be Clark. "I want to leave you with one word."

"I've got a couple of choice words for you," Clark says.

"Lycanthropy," says the mean doctor.

Wow, that's a big word, and it makes the man on

the floor look really amazed. "That's...That's not possible," he says. "You've proven...? But how?"

And then he looks at me.

There is a whir whir as the curtain covering the window opens and suddenly I feel tingly all over. It feels like the moonlight is setting little fires on my skin. They do not hurt though, they just feel kind of itchy.

I look at my hands, which are the most itchy and there is more hair there than ever there was before. It is thick and gray, sprouting so fast it does not even make sense. My bones are popping loud. It feels good, like when I crack my knuckles even though Doctor Brown says it is a nasty habit.

"Clark?" I say. My face feels tight. "What is lycanthropy?" My voice sounds funny because my teeth are getting all big. I touch them and they are sharp.

"Astrid," Clark says. His voice is quiet, but fast. Like he is telling me a secret. "Astrid, stay with me."

"I am right here," I say. But everything in the world is starting to look funny, all black and white like. And I am hungry. So hungry. I have never felt this hungry in my whole entire life.

"Astrid, you're a—"

And then it is almost like his voice turns off. Or he is still saying things, but I cannot understand him anymore. I cannot understand anything anymore except that I need to eat something now and there on the other side of the room there is One Soft Thing, and my teeth are so sharp. I leap from the bed and stare at the Soft Thing. I smell the Soft Thing.

My clothes are so tight and they are ripping and tearing and the Soft Thing is making a whole lot of noise, but I am big and it is small. I stand tall on four legs, and my tail helps me balance. I can hear my four feet click with claws on the hard, cold floor, even over the sounds the Soft Thing is making.

My ears push back, and I snarl.

The Soft Thing is stupid. It does not protect all the squishy soft parts of its body. It only tries a little to protect its throat, its face. I do not want to go there. I dive forward and bury my long snout in its warm belly.

I can feel and not just hear all the loud sounds it makes then, as I rip away the cloth and flesh, swallowing it down at once. I dive in again. My clawed feet press hard against the Soft Thing's legs and hold it still as I tear it to pieces.

After a long time, it stops trying to move and waits. Then it stops trying to breathe and dies.

Then there are only bones left. I chew and crack them against my hard, strong teeth. The Soft Thing is no longer soft, but barren and brittle.

When I look up, the moon has almost sunk below the window. And then it has. My bones sink back into place, and my body grows smaller. My fur sinks back into my skin.

I can hear the speakers. Someone is saying my name. There are a strange man's bones in my mouth and someone is saying my name.

I scream and scream and scream until they have to make me go to sleep, just as the sun is coming up.

Then it is another morning after. I wake up naked, dirty with blood. Not my blood, though. Clark's blood.

Doctor Brown does not come back again. I think he was in trouble after he helped me. I'm not sorry he helped me, but I will never ask again. I just will let the new doctor give me my shot, and I will forget to ask where the blood comes from, that is not mine. I will take a bath instead. I will take a bath and remember the last word I heard before everything broke.

Lycanthropy. Lycanthropy. Lycanthropy.

Could it be that such a long word just stands for another morning after?

* * *

Ria Hill is a writer, librarian, and definitely not a serial killer living in NYC. When not creating unusual characters and strange situations, they can typically be found at the library, slinging James Patterson books. They love reading, knitting, playing the ukulele (badly), and spending time with their spouse. Someday, when the plague is at an end, they will sing karaoke again. Find them online at riahill.weebly.com and on Twitter @RiaWritten.

Aegir The Mariner

by Joseph S. Samaniego

Aegir the Mariner

By Joseph S. Samaniego

The evening was warm when Aegir and his best friend, Elindul, were drinking ale in the tavern just up from the docks. The two grey-haired men toasted their shared adventures and laughed at stories from their youth.

"It's been a good life, Aegir," Elindul smiled, taking a sip of his tankard.

"Aye, it has been," Aegir smiled. "Sixty some years we've sailed these waters and for sixty years we've returned to these shores."

"Long ago were the days when we'd boarded those longships with Haakon, Fenrir, and good king Theodorif," Elindul nodded.

A solemn silence crept over the two men.

"A righteous king indeed, gods rest his soul in the halls of Ymir, fighting and drinking for the rest of eternity." Aegir said, raising his tankard high in a toast.

Elindul clanked his tankard with Aegir's.

The two drank large gulps of their ale, wiped the suds from their greying beards, and sighed contently.

"You didn't bring me here to talk about the old days, did you?" Elindul said, looking at his friend.

Aegir smirked. "No, I didn't."

"Spit it out then."

Aegir leaned close to whisper. "I want to go on one more adventure," Aegir said.

Elindul rolled his eyes. "We're old. Our time has passed, Aegir."

"Maybe it has, but what if we have one more exciting tale in us?" Aegir responded. "Don't you remember our first voyage together?"

Elindul sighed and leaned back in his chair with a smile. "Aye, I do indeed."

* * *

It was a warm, sunny morning when Aegir pushed off from the dock of Furgelsound, sailing aboard his small longship with a crew of six. Just enough of a crew to sail off into the unknown for the first time. A new sailor by his side, a young man from a neighboring jarldom named Elindul.

Aegir himself wasn't that much older or experienced, but the young captain had taken to the sea, and now was his chance to prove his worth with his first voyage as captain of his own ship.

"Pull the long line, tighten the sail!" He ordered.

Aegir stood at the stern of the ship, as all captains would, watching his men with careful eyes. He was impressive at six foot five inches, just over four rods of Gota measurement.

His crew pulled the hemp rope taunt and wrapped it around a wooden peg.

Elindul sat in his position, ready to row. Aegir grinned at the new sailor.

"First time aboard a ship?" Aegir asked, his dark hair framing his face.

He pulled it back and tied it in a warrior's knot. Like others, his sides were knife shaved to the skin.

Elindul nodded. "Yes, captain. I'm wanting to see the world."

"We will," Aegir smiled. "It's time to explore the seas!"

The ship sailed north, uncharted territories for the young sailors. It was a place full of fables and sea monsters. North of Eire was a sea full of mystery. Aegir, having been a sailor on other ships, rowing for other captains, had dreamed of seeing the northern sea.

Those other captains had their minds set on plunder, but Aegir wanted more. He wanted to unlock something. That is why only six other men volunteered when he had presented his small ship. A durable ship he had constructed himself.

Elindul had been traveling to the hold when he heard of the crazy captain wanting to sail north. The captain that had never led men before. Now, that was an adventure if he had ever heard of one.

Days went on as the men rowed through the morning and during the doldrums, but then sailed with haste as the winds picked up. Aegir gripped the main line, pulled at the steerboard rudder, guiding his trusty ship over rough seas.

Storms picked up as the air grew colder, biting the men with icy teeth. Aegir pulled the sail up, directed his men to row, hold, and row again over waves and rough seas. Each man seeing firsthand that Aegir was not a man that was crazy but gifted on the seas.

"We sail north and find glory!" Aegir yelled out over the roaring of the winds and waves.

The seas were relentless throughout the seventh night. A foreboding torrent on a vast expanse of nothingness. Storm clouds above the sailors and a dark sea that was only visible when the lightning cracks through the clouds gave way to tall waves crashing around them.

"Brace yourselves!" Aegir shouted.

He looked out, the sea stared back. It wasn't a sea he had ever seen before. No, this was an angry, evil sea. The waves broke high.

Aegir saw faces of demons and spirits within the waves. Ghastly images that would haunt sailors through their years. He, like all sailors, had heard of the tales of the sea ghosts.

Rain poured down on the ship and waves surrounding them. The spirits wanted Aegir and his crew to join them. Bones in the ocean, it was called.

Aegir was determined to reach the northern sea and see what a treacherous journey was worth.

Elindul, gripping the ship's side rail, made his way to the captain. Aegir steadied himself.

"Elindul," Aegir said to the young man. "Ready the oars and help me bring us back to true."

Elindul stared at Aegir. "Was that..."

"Aye, it was. They'll be around us in storms like this. Seas have a way of bringing the ghosts to the surface. Hold fast, brother," Aegir said, clasping Elindul's shoulder.

The young, fresh-faced sailor stumbled over to the seats and made ready the oars. Aegir smiled as his sailor did as he was told.

They rowed against the coming waves, their ship lifting high, and then pulled down, directly down. The sailor's gripped the rails and mask as tightly as they could, knuckles whitening with pressure. The ship dropped straight down a nearly hundred-foot monster of a wave.

"Hold fast, men! Hold fast or we dine in Helisn's hall tonight!" Aegir cried out.

The ship hit the trough of the wave with a huge creak and bump, bouncing each man a foot into the air. A cheer rang out, but Aegir calmed them.

"Here it comes again! Row, you marvelous bastards, and we'll be heroes when we reach home again!" Aegir laughed as another gigantic wave pulled the ship high again.

Elindul rowed with all his might, as did the others, while Aegir held the steerboard with a tight grip.

Blood seeped out from under his palms, coating the wood with a red stain.

"This sea wants us bound in bones! We've insulted the gods and there's a devil to pay!" a sailor cried out as the wave dropped the ship down again.

Aegir scoffed. "This is nothing. No gods or devils give a damn about you, Hafgot!" Aegir laughed. "We're fools and foolhardy! The gods overlook us, and so we sail under their feet and steal their gold and women!"

Just then, the ship hit the trough of the wave again with a mighty bounce. Another wave crashed on the ship, pouring water over the men, but the wave didn't lift them in the air, nor sent them towering above the sea. Aegir looked out and smiled.

"The worst is behind us, men. Good sailing!" Aegir laughed.

The men cheered as the weather cleared around them. The men pounded the wooden ship rails with their fists, singing in old Gota.

"Vi seiler for hjem, for kvinner, for gull og ære. Vi seglar till helvetet finner oss gamla och gråa!"

Aegir smiled and laughed at his men's joyous reaction. It was a victory over the ocean, a foe that could never really be defeated. The sea will always win the war, no matter how many battles a captain will win.

Days later, along calm waters, Aegir looked out over the still sea. For the winter season, the sun was above them, midday, but faint to their eyes.

The air was frosty, near or even below freezing,

depending on the wind. The sailors had donned their fur coats made from deer, bear, or seal.

Aegir peered through the clouds, aligning his quartz sun spar stone with the wooden sundisk, trying to get his ship's heading. Elindul joined Aegir on the port side rail. Snow was falling, and just under the horizon, Aegir spied the encroaching sea ice creeping south for its seasonal migration.

"It's calm, ain't it, captain?" Elindul asked.

"Aye, too calm." Aegir sucked in a breath. "It's said Sjöorm swims these waters. He likes the cold."

"Sjöorm?"

"A serpent of ice and death, swimming savage seas near the ice flows. He's out there, and that's why we're here." Aegir grinned.

"You brought us here to fight Sjöorm?" Elindul asked, his mouth agape.

Aegir patted him on his shoulder. "What else is up here in the frozen lands? Not a damn thing, but dead things. I don't want to deal with the dead, those restless bones." Aegir shivered. "No, Sjöorm is the prize to show everyone back in Furgelsound."

A lone wave crested the surface of the sea. Another wave followed, and then a closer one still.

Aegir looked out over the waves, growing in number and size. He grabbed his spear.

"The beast comes," he said, tightening his grip.

The other sailors had but a moment before a raging sea serpent, roaring with a booming voice, broke from the surface and towered over the ship.

"Here it comes!" one sailor cried out.

The serpent rushed forward with a massive head down to the ship, scooping the sailor in its mighty maw. Thousands of teeth clenched down, slicing the man in two.

"Spread out!" Aegir ordered.

The sailors did as instructed, leaving a gap between each other. The monster lunged forward again. This time, it met with a fierce spear tip from Aegir.

The iron spike pierced the beast's jaw, but it just tossed the spear into the sea. Aegir quickly grabbed another spear, while the beast took aim at another sailor. This time, the serpent caught its target.

Elindul nocked an arrow to his bow and let loose, catching the serpent in the right eye. Blood oozed from the wound. Elindul fired another arrow, grazing the beast as it dove under the waves.

"It's swimming away!" a sailor shouted in triumph.

Aegir silenced him and the others. "Quiet you fools! It's coming back."

The beast roared up from behind Aegir as he waited for a moment along the starboard side. Aegir quickly turned. Elindul let loose more arrows, and the others stabbed with spears. Aegir took aim and hurled his iron tipped spear at the serpent. The spear sailed true, lodging itself into the neck of the beast.

"The underside is soft! Aim there or for the eyes!" Aegir yelled out.

Arrows flew, piercing the flesh under Sjöorm's jaw. Aegir gripped his axe and lined up the beast. Aegir's axe, handed down from his father, was a mere hatchet

18

used by sailors for generations. It could be rope, meat, and wood. Now Aegir needed it to cut Sjöorm's flesh.

Aegir saw the beast lunge forward, and he saw his opportunity. Aegir jumped from the ship and onto the beast. Gripping the scales, Aegir held on with his axe in his right hand.

He made a move to grip the horn of the beast, and with a mighty blow, Aegir chopped down on the beast with his trusty axe.

Again, he thrusted the axe down onto the serpent's skull. Again, and again, and as many times as his arm had the strength to hold the axe.

The serpent wobbled, feeling each blow with increasing force until a large gash had opened in its head, pouring blood down its sides.

The beast lumbered towards the ship. Aegir brought his axe down for good measure, dropping the serpent's head to the ship. Aegir jumped off.

"The beast is dead," the captain panted.

The men cheered. Elindul grabbed another axe and hacked at the serpent's neck. Others took turns when one tired out. Aegir took the final turn, and after six hours of chopping, Sjöorm's head finally separated from his body.

Aegir smiled, along with his men, as they bounded the enormous head in a cow hide tarp and tied it with a rope.

"A fine gift for King Sven!" Aegir cheered.

It was a sunny day with Aegir's small longship, crewed by four stout, but weary men sailed into the fjord and further down to the harbor of Furgelsound. A crowd gathered, growing as rumors of the Sjöorm's head spread around the town. Aegir hopped off the ship, hoisting the massive head, with help from Elindul, on his back.

The weary captain carried it to the longhouse of King Sven. Such a sight amazed the grizzled old king and his three warrior sons. The king ordered the head boiled and the skull to be mounted above his throne.

The men were hailed as heroes, their fallen brothers honored and celebrated. Mead and ale flowed as the festival went on for two weeks.

Aegir and his crew had brought back proof of their voyage to the icy, deadly northern sea. An ocean of monsters and fraught with terrors beyond most human's imagination. It was a voyage that earned him the moniker of the Mariner, a name he wore with pride, no matter how many voyages he sailed.

* * *

"You really want to go back out there?" Elindul asked, his eyebrow raised.

Aegir sighed. "I see it in my dreams."

"You see what?"

"Sjöorm. He calls to me." Aegir said.

"He is dead. We killed him." Elindul shook his head.

Aegir nodded. "Aye, and now it is time for one more voyage to meet our old foe out there on the icy waters."

Elindul nodded. "One last adventure to match our first."

"Just like our first." Aegir smiled and winked.

Joseph S. Samaniego is a fantasy writer who started off as a fan of the fantasy genre and decided to begin telling his own tales. He has been publishing his stories since 2016 and have published ten books thus far. In 2020, Joseph started his own publishing company, Mage's Moon Publishing, in an effort to build on his own writing and to hopefully be able to help others in the near future. His goal is to one day become a full time writer and publisher.

ROUGH AND TUMBLE

by Bryson Richard

Rough and Tumble

By Bryson Richard

Sawney's fingers reeked of shit as he drove them into Davidson's nostrils, and Davidson recalled having seen the man reach into his britches numerous times and dig at whatever wet wilderness lay in the canyon of his ass.

Davidson thrashed his head, but Sawney held him from behind, coiled his other arm around his neck and flexed. The bulge of Sawney's bicep cut into Davidson's windpipe, rendering him still. Sawney hooked his fingers into Davidson's nostrils, turning his nose into a snout, and peeled his head back roughly.

Around them, the crowd roared. Davidson was aware of excited faces and the jingle of coins as wagers were brandished, aware of all the instructions and obscenities being screamed at him, aware, but it was the awareness of a dream.

He blew air and saliva through his gaping mouth and felt the pressure of Sawney's thumb on his temple. He winced at the knife-like edge of the nail and knew what was happening seconds before it happened. The nail, an inch long, thick, and with a black crescent of filth under the outer edge, slid to Davidson's left eye.

"They love this part." Sawney breathed down over his face.

The thumb darted, the nail penetrated the seam of the eyelid, and with a quick torque, Davidson's eyeball tumbled from its socket, the optic nerve unraveling behind it.

It plopped against his cheek like a wet tea bag.

* * *

If you'd asked James Davidson earlier in the day why he struggled to fit in among the miners, he'd probably point to his face and shrug. The warm, watery brown eyes, the dimpled chin, the regally long nose, and the fashionable sideburns contrasted the disheveled and sullen visages of the miners.

It was also his profession as the schoolmaster, that greatest of all punching bags, which made him so unlikable to the villagers of Highgate. There was a point of suspicion about him. They all agreed, in his dress, mannerisms, and words, in his vocation, and the awkwardness with which he interacted with them.

He wasn't much out of boyhood himself. Why was he spending his time with books and parchments,

24

quill, and ink, when he could be out fighting, fucking, and making money, like other men?

The most striking of slights was that Mr. Davidson didn't include the bible in his teachings. Instead, he focused on poetry, handwriting, and arithmetic. Some whispered he was after their daughters. Others, who'd taken to referring to him as *Dapper Davidson*, feared it was their sons he preferred.

Regardless, it mattered not to the villagers that the young schoolmaster from the north was invited, *hired* even, by the mining company they all worked for.

Even their children had no respect for him, as none had bothered to report to school.

Instead, Thomas Bernath, one of the foremen, stood in the doorway of the dark schoolhouse, dressed for work. He'd taken a detour on his way to the mine.

"It's quite simple," Thomas said and removed his three-cornered hat. "You owe Sawney Roberts a fight."

Davidson's eyes darted around the small, dark interior of the schoolhouse.

"And not just any fight, but a rough and tumble." Thomas continued. He held his hat before him, gripped the brim, but whether in excitement or nervousness, Davidson couldn't tell.

"What's a rough and tumble?"

"Means there's no rules." Thomas said.

"But why? Why would Sawney Roberts want to fight me?"

"Word spread 'bout what you said." Thomas's tone

25

implied it should have been obvious. "Folks 'round here take insult to heart. You've tainted Sawney's honor, offended him. Now he's challenged you to a rough and tumble."

"That's ridiculous." Davidson gulped.

"It's how things are done 'round here."

Davison recalled making a small quip the previous day, but nothing that warranted a duel.

He'd been with his twelve grubby, sinewy pupils, and they were looking upon him with slack jaws and disinterested faces, as always. They showed little inclination towards learning, ignored him, talked amongst themselves, became combative when he tried to correct them.

By day's end, he was as uninterested in them as they were him. In fact, he was ashamed to admit, he'd become downright antagonistic towards them, out of sheer boredom and spite.

During his lesson on weights and balances, the students went off on a tangent about strength, specifically which of their fathers was strongest. This then extended to the other miners, namely one Sawney Roberts, who all agreed was the strongest.

Davidson knew the man. Had seen him in the village, a fearsome, savage looking fellow, with thick black hair and beard and only one darting eye; the other, the right eye, a flattened wad of skin with a dark slit that had once held an eyeball. Sharpened yellow incisors hooked over his bottom lip and into his beard, and, strangest of all, he kept the nails on his thumbs long, like talons.

The discussion among the children of just how strong this man-beast was, eventually reached ridiculous levels of inaccuracy and distraction, and Davidson told them as much.

"Let's focus more on the lesson and not on some louts' imagined ability to lift two full barrels of beer over his head."

"I seen't it happen!" One cross-eyed boy shouted.

"I believe he could toss you over his head, Mr. Davidson." A dirty faced girl grinned.

"I believe I'll toss each of you over *my* head and off this damned mountain unless you silence yourselves." He glared at them, at their simple, expressionless faces. "Sawney Roberts can go lift a bucket of water over his rotten self, might do something about the stink. And the lot of you can recite your letters before I begin a rash of knuckle whacks." He brandished a switch made from a green sapling, more like a whip than a club.

"You ought not say that 'bout Sawney." The crossed eyed boy said.

Davidson whacked his knuckles and let that be his final comment on the subject, or so he thought.

Now, in the schoolhouse with Thomas Bernath, Davidson tried to straighten his posture, lift his chin, but the act came off as much too forced. "I... I refuse the challenge." He stuttered.

Thomas's eyes bulged. "You mean you won't meet him?" It appeared the idea was unheard of.

"Of course not. I'm a schoolmaster, not a pugilist."

"But he's saying the most horrible things about

you, sir. Your own good name is on the line here." Thomas took a cautious step into the school, "And I'm afraid if you don't meet his challenge, well, he might just come looking for you. Might even come here, to the schoolhouse. It wouldn't be decent for children to see something like that."

Davidson's legs shook. He sat abruptly on the students' bench. "Surely the constable wouldn't allow such things." He whimpered.

"Oh, him?" Thomas scratched his neck distractedly. "Shep Roberts is Sawney's big brother. Don't expect much help from him."

Davidson found himself unable to meet Thomas's gaze, even though the man stood as a silhouette against the open door. Outside late spring was giving over to early summer and the brightness of the day and the vibrance of the greenery contrasted the dark, sooty interior of the school just as Thomas Bernath's easy, matter-of-fact delivery of the challenge contrasted the growing dread blooming in Davidson's mind.

"Word has spread. There are wagers being taken already. If you don't meet the challenge, you're looking at upsetting a lot more folks than just Sawney Roberts."

"Wagers?" Davidson balked.

"People'r already gathering down by Meadow Creek. Little early if you ask me. Sawney won't be back from the mine until suppertime."

"Who in their right mind would bet on me winning?"

"Oh, you misunderstand, sir. It's not about you winning. It's about the damage you're going to take."

"Damage?"

"Yes sir. Is he going to bite off your nose, or rip your lips, or chew some fingers." Thomas held up his right hand, which Davidson saw was missing the index and middle finger down to the second knuckle, "Or maybe even snatch one of your eyes?" Thomas nodded grimly. "That's what most folks want, the eye gouging. But any kind of maiming, disfiguring, and mutilation are in order."

Davidson blinked.

"I thought someone should make you aware." Thomas said. "Being new to these parts and all, I just don't think it's fair sport."

"Please." Tears spilled from Davidson's eyes, and he wiped them away hurriedly before turning to Thomas, "Please. You must help me. What do I do?"

"Well," Thomas took a few steps into the school, "You ever been in a fight?"

* * *

Davidson didn't know if he'd fought free of Sawney's grip or if the big, dark-haired miner had simply let him go. Free for the moment, he reached up and prodded the eyeball that flopped against his face. He was terribly disoriented.

The eye hurt, of course, but he was simultaneously seeing the swath of dirty, pebble strewn ground they

29

fought on, and the delighted, red faces of the roaring crowd.

They loved it, gestured animatedly, jostled each other. Spittle flew from their lips as they screamed insults, instructions, or the obvious observation that his eyeball was hanging out of its socket. Most held flagons of rum or whiskey.

Sawney stretched a hand towards them, and someone shoved a flagon into it. He drank greedily, let the alcohol dribble over the edges of his mouth and down his black beard and trickle through the thick, curled fibers of his chest hair. Grinning, he thrust his wet torso forward and smashed a fist against it, roared like a beast.

"He's far too dapper to grapple with me!" Sawney caught sight of the slick of blood on his thumb-talon and slipped it into his mouth, sucked it clean.

The audience thundered their approval.

Meanwhile, Davidson struggled with stuffing his eyeball back into his head; the damned thing kept tumbling out like it didn't fit, didn't belong. He swallowed a surge of vomit, but his bisected vision caused a swirl of nausea that he couldn't combat.

He whipped his head to the side and spewed a mixture of stomach acid, rum, and blood, whipped his head with such force the dangling organ swung through the air and smacked against his ear.

Both the crowd and Sawney erupted in laughter.

Falling to his knees, Davidson dug the eyeball and length of exposed nerve out of his thatch of sideburns, and simply held onto it, unsure of what else to do.

Pointing, chuckling, Sawney approached the stooped over schoolmaster. He bucked his hips at the back of Davidson's head, then turned towards the crowd and raised his arms in the air victoriously, bathing in their approval.

Davidson let go of his eyeball, leaving it to rest on his cheek, and reeled to face Sawney, fully intending to announce his surrender. He pawed at Sawney's chest, tried to utter words of submission but only stuttered incomprehensibly.

His hands slid down the miner's bare belly and grasped at Sawney's britches with such force they split at the seam running up the inner thigh.

Sawney's great hairy balls dangled out of his britches and the crowd went wild.

* * *

"Don't worry about form or posture or even what's *fair*." Thomas Bernath said earlier.

They'd hunkered down in the empty schoolhouse, the door still open to let in the daylight and fresh air.

"It's not about that. There are no points, no arbitrators, just the two of you fellas going at it until one of you can't go no more." He drank from a tankard full of spirits, and Davidson followed suit. "The temptation to be merciful will gnaw at you as surely as the good Lord made you, but you must ignore it. You got to, 'cause Sawney won't be merciful to you." Thomas filled the tankards. "Although, I'm inclined to believe he might... Play with you."

Davidson frowned.

Thomas shrugged uncomfortably. "I don't mean this to be disrespectful, but you're not the most imposing man, physically speaking. The consensus is that Sawney's going to rag you like a wild dog in a hare's nest. But folks like spectacle, and Sawney's a known rough and tumbler. Hell, he makes double his wages from the mines on the fights."

"So, you're saying I'm a dead man." Davidson sighed.

"No. Folks don't die in a rough and tumble. It's not about taking a life, it's about taking a trophy, and leaving a mark."

Davidson's eyes flicked down to Thomas' missing fingers.

"He keeps his thumb nails long so he can scoop out eyeballs, and he's filed some teeth down to fangs to bite off noses, lips, and fingers, but even Sawney's lost a time or two." Thomas tapped his right eye.

"I wondered about that." Davidson said, and for the first time there was something close to optimism in his voice.

Thomas nodded gravely, "I saw that fight. Sawney had it out for some scrawny northerner who'd wandered down this way and was laboring in the mines. Can't remember his name, only that he was a lumberjack from up around Ohio. Folks think he got in trouble – fucked a wife, stole a horse, spent money, all of which weren't his. He was a desperate wretch when he showed up here. Seemed like an easy target, I suppose, 'specially to someone like Sawney, who's always looking for another notch on his club, figuratively speaking. Anyway, unpleasantries were exchanged, and they had a rough and tumble lined up in quick order."

Thomas glanced at Davidson's tankard, picked up the bottle to fill it, but Davidson slide it away.

"No. I don't think I need anymore. It's certainly calmed me enough, or at least numbed me to my impending doom."

Thomas lowered the bottle. "It might make you sloppy, but a rough and tumble is supposed to be sloppy. Besides, a little numbness, under the circumstances, might be the best thing for you."

Davidson eyed the bottle for a moment, then slide his tankard forward.

Thomas nodded curtly, poured, and continued his story.

"Everyone expected Sawney to make a spectacle, and he did, at first. He pounded away at that lumberjack, yanked him by his hair and beard, stomped him, threw him around. But when Sawney bit down on the fella's fingers the unexpected happened: Quick as lighting that lumberjack snatched Sawney's eye with his free hand, like those fingers were coated in butter. Just slipped into the socket and plucked his peeper like you would a grape from the vine." Thomas shrugged. "Darndest thing. Sawney didn't feel much like fighting after that."

Davidson sat quietly, unable to think over the roar

of anxiety in his mind, gnawing away at his nerves, at his emotions, at his very soul.

Thomas smiled. "You know something? Now that I retell it, I have the idea that that lumberjack might have planned it all along. Seems reasonable to think. Folks didn't know him all that well, so they made some assumptions based on his frame and build. And perhaps he was counting on that. Maybe even spent the whole fight losing, knowing he was going to win. All he did was bide his time and take a beating. Sometimes that's not so bad. Sometimes it's all a man can do is take a beating."

Davidson held his tankard in both hands and studied Thomas carefully. "You've shown me a kindness I'd not expected in this place."

Thomas gave him a thin smile, lifted his own tankard in salute. "Well, you're just accustomed to kinder places. And that's another thing. If you don't meet the challenge, you'll have to leave, and I mean immediately, willingly, or not, folks will see to it that you're gone."

"There's no place to go." Davidson sighed, implying a long, miserable story. "Alas, much like your lumberjack from Ohio, I'm out of options. Highgate, the contract with the company, it's really my last chance. If I don't make it here, I won't make it at all."

Thomas nodded slowly, finished his rum, then repeated himself. "Sometimes all a man can do is take a beating."

* * *

Davidson surveyed the crowed with his remaining eye, embarrassingly aware of Sawney's stinking, sweltering genitals inches from his face. He was dismayed by how many of the miners and their families were present.

Children he knew from the schoolhouse and pretty much the entire citizenry of Highgate, North Carolina. Thomas Bernath had lied in this regard, it seemed. Even Shep Roberts, the constable, was attending.

"I think he's after a taste of the old eggs and sausage!" Sawney shouted to the crowd's great glee.

A sudden and immediate calm swept over Davidson as the vision in his left eye clouded, darkened, then ended altogether. The eyeball, the nerve, something was damaged, and he would never again gain its use.

Gritting his teeth, and without knowing he was going to do it, Davidson reached out and grasped Sawney's testicles. They were large, bulky, covered in kinks of dark hair, like every other inch of the man.

Sawney froze.

The crowd died and zeroed in on this single action.

The combatants' eyes met. Davidson — bent over, eyeball dangling from the weepy red hole in his face, the other blurry with tears of pain, humiliation, and flickering rage — glared into Sawney's one eye which bulged grotesquely from his meaty red face, spittle foaming at the corners of his mouth, afraid to move or twitch or even breathe. Words appeared on the miner's lips but were not spoken.

"Give 'em a tug!" a woman hollered from somewhere in the hushed crowed.

Sporadic, mean humored chuckles spread among the spectators.

Sawney looked into the crowd. They'd never actually seen the expression on his face before, but he appeared to be pleading, silently begging them to interfere, to stop the fight before it went any further.

Davidson, meanwhile, didn't loosen his hold for a second.

"Twist 'em off!" Another voice from the crowd, but Davidson wasn't sure if it was a woman's voice or a man's or even from which direction it had come, or if he'd only heard it in his head.

He squeezed firmly.

Sawney pulled back at the waist and swung a fist at Davidson's face.

Davidson lowered his head, absorbed the panicked blow with the top of his skull, and squeezed Sawney's balls harder.

Sawney screeched, went rigid and toppled over onto the dusty ground.

Davidson, who kept hold of the scrotum, tumbled over with him.

The crowd let out a collective gasp.

Sawney remained still, his one eye clamped shut, his face a contortion of pain, covered in dirt, while Davidson lay tangled in the miner's legs and fought to right himself with one hand, the other still grasping the sack tightly.

"Rip 'em off!" An excited cry. The crowd resurrected with a roar. The jangle of coins commenced.

Sawney, perhaps seeing the way things had turned against him, or simply because he was in such physical pain, he had to be free of the clamped fist, finally tried to beat Davidson away. He rained punches, pulled at the scrawny man's hair, used his fingers as claws and racked them against his neck and shoulders, leaving jagged red trails in the pale skin of the schoolmaster. Davidson took it all, remained calm, committed, his grip firm.

Keeping his chin tucked towards his boney chest, his right eyeball covered in dirt and grime and dangling uselessly before him, Davidson squeezed as tightly as he could, the testicles gathering at the bottom of his fist like the knotted end of a rope. Then he pulled, pulled as folks in a far-off future he would never witness will pull cords to start their lawn mowers. He yanked once, twice, the third time there seemed to be a give in whatever ligaments kept everything in place down there, and Sawney yowled like a big cat.

Another yank, then another, and suddenly Davidson toppled over. Sawney went rigid again, his face nearly purple; he hadn't drawn a breath since Davidson had started pulling. A high, childish whine slipped from the burley miner's hidden lips. Then he turned his head and vomited into the dirt. His one eye rolled to the white, closed, and Sawney was unconscious.

Davidson sat up, glanced at the mass of bloody

flesh gripped in his right hand, then tossed it into the dirt, uninterested in the contents of the scrotum. He stumbled up to his feet, eyeball twitching, pendulum like with the motion. He lurched forward through the crowd. Most parted willingly for him.

A few slapped him on the back, smirked and congratulated him, but he ignored it all, save the smile and applause of Thomas Bernath, who appeared among the dirty, simple faces.

"Well done, my boy!" Thomas cheered.

Davidson reached a hand towards him, intending to ask for a drink of water. He was desperately thirsty, but pitched over instead, sprawling into the tall grass on the banks of Meadow Creek, also, blissfully unconscious.

* * *

Sawney Roberts changed over the years. He never regained the glory of being the most prolific rough and tumbler of the area, or, as some used to claim, the entire state. He became tame, quiet, developed breasts, and descended into a profound depression after being let go from the mine.

He left Highgate, never to return.

Once, a handbill from a traveling circus was circulated among the miners. It advertised the bearded woman of the sideshow. Powders, rouge, and eye paint were used to smooth out her otherwise rough and masculine complexion, and her thick hair and beard were done in ribbons and bows. Her exposed breasts, heavy masses of flesh cradled in her arms, were covered in coarse curls of hair.

It was agreed by most that she looked uncannily like Sawney Roberts, until his brother Shep got his hands on the flyer and made it disappear.

As for Davidson, he adjusted to life as a one-eyed schoolmaster rather well. His students regarded him with a newfound luster. Several of them had witnessed the rough and tumble and regaled those who'd been punished with parents capable of good sense with the gory details.

The rest of the villagers were warmer to him. For many years afterward, and frequently, folks approached him, shook his hand, grinned, and wanted to discuss the rough and tumble. He tended to let them do most of the talking. The truth was, he didn't have much of a recollection of the whole thing. Only a lingering sense of revulsion at the sensation of ripping flesh from a living body like one would onions from a garden bed.

* * *

Bryson Richard is from the Black Swamp region of Ohio. He writes short stories but has been plucking away at some longer pieces. Some of his stories have appeared in *What One Wouldn't Do*, an anthology edited by Scott J. Moses, *Mother: Tales of Love and Terror* from Weird Little Worlds, and *Step into the Light* an anthology from Bag of Bones Press.

Breath of Fresh Air
by Rae Lucero

Breath of Fresh Air

By Rae Lucero

I look up at the ticking clock and watch as the seconds pass by. As the time draws near, I feel more and more anxious. I know it won't be that bad and I know I should be more excited than scared, but I just can't help but dread the pain. I'm just hoping that this will go by quickly.

After what feels like an eternity, the alarm finally goes off. Our instructor stands.

"Alright class, that's us. Single file line, just like we practiced."

We all stand, leaving everything in the room, and walk single file out of the classroom. Our class walks all the way down a long corridor, into the general medical room, and joins the lines that are set up.

As the group ahead of us finishes up, the first of the kids in my class start to get their injections. I take a step forward. The first girl seems to hardly notice, but the boy in the next booth winces and rubs at his arm for a full minute. Another step forward.

I can see that one nurse is trying to tell a kid something, but can't quite hear what she's saying over the nervous chatter of the classmates around me. Our instructor has been trying to keep us quiet, but we have all been too on edge to be as well behaved as usual.

Another step forward and I'm next. My eyes are stuck to the nurse as she finishes with the girl in front of me and prepares for my injection. I take a deep breath.

I can do this.

This is what I've been wanting for so long. One more step. Fear causes my legs to remain frozen in place. I force myself to step up to the booth and sit in the chair, waiting for me.

The nurse wipes my arm with an alcohol wipe and grabs the needle. It's bigger than I thought it would be and I can't look away. I know I should, but I can't help it. I watch, wide eyed, as the nurse jabs the needle into my arm and pushes the plunger down.

The purple liquid enters my arm and my veins immediately feel like they've been set on fire. Shock and pain overtake me and my ears start to ring. The nurse pulls the enormous needle from my skin and covers the injection site with a cotton ball.

She murmurs something, but my ears are still ringing and I'm way too distracted by the fire raging in my bloodstream to try to understand. The nurse nods at the cotton ball. I grab a hold of it and stare back at the nurse. She is pointing to the next kid and I realize she's telling me to move along.

I lift myself from the chair and slowly walk away from the injection booth to join the rest of my classmates that are done. A few of them are crying, most are rubbing their arms. I just stand there holding the cotton ball as the fire slowly subsides and my ears finally stop ringing.

The fire is replaced by a dull ache that isn't so bad, much more bearable. I throw the cotton ball away and wait in silence as the last of my class finishes up. Once everyone is done, we head back to class, and the lesson resumes right where it left off.

After we finish lessons for the day, I head to the station lobby to look out the big windows. For the last few years, I've been doing this, watching as people enjoy their scheduled time outside. I've been dreaming of the day that I would finally be eligible to go out onto the planet's surface, and now it's only a few days away.

Only a week's worth of injections and I will be able to go outside for the first time. The pain is nothing compared to the excitement of being able to go outside. My whole life has been inside the white walls of the station, but I've always kept my eyes on what was outside.

Humans have only been on this planet for about seventy-five years. The process of terraforming is slow, so they had to come up with a way for people to be able to go outside in the meantime: that's why they made the injection. Now that I'm old enough to get the injections, I will finally be able to go outside for the first time in my life.

The next day's injection is much easier. This time, I turn my head away. Not seeing the giant needle helps to lessen the anxiety. The fire in my veins rages, but knowing it won't last long makes it seem to go faster. After the third injection, I'm much more confident.

It's quicker for the whole class as everyone is getting used to it. Much less crying and everyone seems to recover pretty much within a minute. As the week goes by, the pain of each injection is replaced with the excitement of my first experience outside.

The morning that we get to go outside, the energy of the class is electric. Everyone is chatting and so excited. The first hour of class is normal lessons, but I can tell that no one is paying attention. Our instructor is trying to get us to focus, but we are all just waiting for injection time and our first trip outside.

When our alarm goes off, the entire class is silent. We walk to the medical room in a perfect line and efficiently make it through the process. We are all just so focused on going outside, being able to feel the sun's light, breathe fresh air, and finally be outside.

Right after the injection, our instructor leads us down several corridors and into the main lobby of the station. We go to the front desk and our instructor checks us in for our appointment time. The receptionist points us towards the airlock and we follow the instructor over to the big door.

The operator has everyone do a bio scan to confirm their identity and outdoor eligibility. Once satisfied, they allow us through the first door, and we wait until the outer doors open.

When the outer doors peel away from each other, a blinding light creeps in around us. The two suns are high in the sky and they cast a warm light all around us that is beaming down brighter than I ever thought possible.

I raise my hand to shield my eyes from the intensity of it. A rush of cold air whirls around us and I take a long, deep breath in. The air smells like nothing I've ever smelled before. It's cool and light, and I can smell fragrant aromas coming from every direction. It's different than I expected.

When I look out into the courtyard, I can see the outside clearer than before. I realize there must be some sort of shade on the station windows because everything is more vibrant than when looking from inside. I follow my class out into the courtyard that surrounds the entire station.

It's filled with many plants, both native and from Earth. We have a greenhouse inside the station, but it mostly houses edible plants: these are decorative. I've only read about them in books and seen them through the shaded windows before. They are much more beautiful up close.

Our instructor tells us we have one hour to explore before we must go back inside. She makes sure that all our watches are set to remind us when time is up. Once we are free to explore, my classmates split into groups and head off in different directions.

I set off alone to take a closer look at all the flowers in a nearby flower bed. As I get close, the smell is so strong and sweet. It's more amazing than anything else I've ever smelled before. I reach for a small yellow flower but at the last second, I stop. I'm not sure if it would even be safe to touch this flower.

We learned about how some plants on this planet are very poisonous to humans and how there are so many that we aren't even sure if all of them are safe. I think about it for a moment and realize there is no way they would let children roam free with dangerous plants around.

I reach again, this time without hesitation, and gently touch the flower. It's soft and delicate. I rub the petals between my fingertips for a few seconds. I could sit here and examine all the beautiful flowers for the rest of the hour, but there is still so much I want to see. Letting the petals fall from my fingers, I take one more sniff of the lovely smell.

I walk to the courtyard fence and look at all that's out there. The planet beyond the fence has remained mostly untouched by humans. The plans to have human settlements all around the planet are slow going.

There are a few bases that are being set up, but the military can only do so much when people can't be outside for too long. I think about all the amazing things the military gets to see and how much time they get to spend outside in the fresh air.

A small gray flying bug lands on the metal fence a few feet away. I take a few careful steps to get closer, being sure not to make too quick of movements or too much noise. The bug is about the size of a blueberry, round head and oval body.

It has antennae sticking out all over its head and six long wings coming from its body. I watch as it crawls up the fence, spreads its wings, and buzzes off. I try to follow its flight, but it moves beyond the fence somewhere and I lose track of it.

I walk along the edge of the courtyard, looking at all the beautiful plants inside the fence and all the wonders of nature outside the fence. Outside the fence there are trees of varying sizes and colors. Tall blue leafed ones, small orange flowered bushes, tall skinny trees with long brown leaves.

There is a stream of water out about twenty-five meters from the fence where there are small native animals. I spot a group of green tailed lizards by it, and watch as they walk by.

Along the fence, I come to another flower bed, this one with big purple flowers. I spend time smelling them all and find a bench nearby to sit on for a while. With my eyes closed, I sit and turn my face to the light of the suns. The rays warm my face and the breeze blow through my hair. I take long deep breaths in and out and enjoy the fresh air.

The sound of my watch alarm going off wakes me from my sun warmed trance. I turn the alarm off and pull myself off the bench. I head in the direction I came from to find my class. An hour already. An hour is much too short to really enjoy being out here. I feel like I was just beginning to explore and now I must go back in and wait until tomorrow.

I see my class up ahead and walk over to join them. We all gathered and then headed to the outer airlock door. As it opens, we walk in and before the door closes to the outside world, I take one more big deep breath to last me until tomorrow, when I get to spend only one more hour outside.

After my classes for the day, I go back to my family's compartment and grab my computer to do some more research about the outside. I try to find pictures of the untouched parts of the planet that I haven't already seen, but the military hasn't released any new ones. Every photo I scroll past was taken by military personnel, and these are just the ones I'm allowed to see.

My whole life, I've wondered what the sun on my skin would feel like. What the breeze through my hair or the rain falling would feel like. Getting to be outside for the allotted hour and having to stay in the courtyard isn't enough for me. The only people who get to venture out of the courtyard and really experience the outside world are the military. If I don't join, then I will never know what it's really like out there. No amount of VR or courtyard time will ever be enough for me. My mind is made up.

I will live on the outside.

* * *

Rae Lucero has always loved storytelling in all mediums, be it TV, movies, books, video games, etc. She believes that storytelling helps connect people to each other and that through stories everyone can experience different perspectives and learn more about their fellow humans. She began writing as a young teen in her free time and has recently begun to pursue writing more seriously. This is her first published short story but definitely not the last.

ANYTHING GOES

by Lexie Carver

Anything Goes

By Lexie Carver

Angelika held the knife high above her head. The blade gleamed as the afternoon sun broke through the hall window. The man, of course, had a name, but Angelika didn't remember it.

He was just the neighbor who'd always wanted to get her alone. He had been watching her since she moved in with her husband. That wasn't important. The task in front of her was. The man was just a stepping stone to sharpen her skills.

She followed him down the long hallway of her home, waiting for the right time to strike. After chatting him up for a while, he'd asked for the restroom. Her first thought was that he was preparing himself for what he thought would be a romantic encounter, but she knew better. She had to do this. It was the only way.

Angelika stepped forward, trying to be silent, but she forgot about the loose floorboard. It creaked loudly under her feet. She froze behind him, arms above her head, too afraid to utter a breath. She saw him slowly turn around, and she quickly hid behind a console table, almost knocking over the lamp on it.

"Shit," she whispered.

She really wasn't cut out for this, but she was a Monroe, and Monroe women were capable of anything. She stayed crouched behind the hideous table that her husband loved, but she always found an eyesore. Well, truth be told, she liked that table now.

After a minute or so, she poked her head out. Seemingly convinced the sound was just the house settling, the man continued walking down the hallway. Careful to step lightly and not make another mistake, Angelika crept behind him, ready to strike at a moment's notice.

Just as she was about to stab him in the back, he stopped abruptly to stare out the window, which, of course, she'd forgotten to close. A butterfly was flying by. Not able to stop her forward momentum, Angelika shoved into him.

The knife clattered and the man's body flew forward down the stairs. His head hit every step with a thump, but none as loud as the thump heard when his head finally hit the polished hardwood floor below.

There was no question the man was dead. One couldn't lose that much blood and live. For a second, Angelika stood transfixed by the scene in front of her in equal parts horror and fascination.

"Damn it. I wanted to stab him. I wanted to see the light leave his eyes. I guess he *is* dead though. My first kill and it was an accident. I am such a klutz. Can't do anything right. I can't tell anyone. My family would just laugh at me, especially my cousin! I'm the only non-murderer in the family. 'Angelika can't even carry out a murder, she'll just accident them to death.' I can hear it now. Now, they'll call it pulling an Angelika." She sighed. "Dead is dead, though. I *did* kill him. I'll get better at this. Right?"

Growling, she stood up and looked down at the body.

"I'm going to have to move him. I can't have him splayed across the foyer. The first thing Harold sees when he comes home is a dead man? That's all I need."

Thinking the task would be easy, Angelika grabbed his arms, hoisting him up. She pulled, but he wouldn't budge. She grunted, putting all of her strength into the task, and managed to move him an inch. Letting out another frustrated growl, she tugged on his arms again and moved him another inch.

This went on for a good hour until she finally moved the body to the kitchen. The pain in her arms and back was a hundred times worse than after her pilates class.

She plopped down on the kitchen stool, her head on the cool marble countertop.

"Murder is a lot harder than it looks."

She was exhausted, but she knew she couldn't stop now. This task had to be finished. And she had to get away with it. To prove to herself that she could do anything she put her mind to, or so she told herself. Reluctantly, she stepped off the rickety, uncomfortable, trendy bar stool.

On still sore legs, she entered the pantry, bent down with a groan, and grabbed her chainsaw from under the loose floorboard in the pantry.

Back in the kitchen, she looked down and realized that half her dress was covered in blood. She shrieked in panic and put down the chainsaw.

Sure, some people might have figured a murder would involve blood or blood splatter and a head injury with a blood pool would make for bloody clothes, but Angelika was never the best at putting two and two together. Also one might wear different clothes for a murder, but again, Angelika was never the best planner.

She stared down at her dress, horrified at the mess — not because she was a fastidious woman or because blood was repellant to her, but because her husband had given her this very dress for their anniversary last year.

How am I going to explain this much blood? I'll have to burn it, destroy it, bury it, do something with it. Harold will need an explanation and he's not an easy man to fool. Ok. A lie. I can do this. OK.

She rubbed her hands together as she continued thinking.

I gave the dress to Marcie, and she spilled wine on it, so I took it to the cleaners and they haven't given it back yet? But why would I lend a dress that

54

means so much to me to Marcie? She can get her own dresses! And then he might ask to pick it up from the cleaners. It's not blood, honey, it's ketchup.

Angelika balled her fists.

Oh, come on! I found an injured animal and ran out to save it? But then where is the animal? That's so depressing. OK. Um... finger paints? I took up painting and forget to wear something to protect the dress. The dry cleaners did it! A laundry accident? None of these works!

Angelika had loved his smarts when they got married. Such an intellectual, a learned man falling for *her*. He was, as her mother put it, "the cat's pajamas and much too good for my Angelika."

It was like a dream come true when they got married, but now it was a noose around her neck. He would ask questions, and she was a terrible liar. She'd have to work on her lying skills next. This lie would be her first big lie since they got married.

OK, first get rid of this guy and then have a long think about which lie to tell.

Angelika ran to her bedroom on the second floor and stood in front of her closet. It was full of designer clothes and luxurious fabrics, but of course, she couldn't change into those. It would have to be some ratty old T-shirt or college sweatshirt, something she owned before she married Harold, something he hadn't bought her.

At least she had the good sense to take off her dress before rummaging around in her closet.

She pulled open several boxes before she found

55

the right one. There were so many keepsakes of the woman she used to be in those boxes, souvenirs of all the things she gave up for marriage, but at least she was able to do what she wanted now. Become the murderer she always wanted to be.

Some kids wanted to be the funniest or the richest when they grew up or the most likely to succeed, but she always wanted to be a murderer, maybe even a serial killer.

Then her bullies wouldn't be laughing at her, they'd respect her as would her family. One has to start somewhere. The other kids saw her as "most likely to mess up everything in life" and she always smiled and took it. Now she was in charge. She would show everyone what she was capable of.

She grabbed her old college sweatshirt and some sweatpants, then put the bloody dress in a bag. She ran down to get something to clean the bloodstains in the bedroom when she saw her own bloody footprints, the blood trail in the foyer, and the now bloody barstool.

"Why am I such an idiot? I'm leaving a bloody trail everywhere! How do you get blood out of a carpet?"

After watching some YouTube videos and a fair amount of cursing, Angelika finally got the blood out of the carpet downstairs, the polished wood in the foyer, the top step on the staircase, and the bar stool in the kitchen. She was out of breath and so exhausted she could faint.

Surely, this was it. She was about to be finished

with all this. If she had known that murder would be so messy with hours of cleanup, she would have laid something down. Although she had no idea what one would lay down.

Maybe she should have searched on the internet for the answers. Or watched something besides a steady stream of romantic comedies. Maybe a horror movie might have clued her in to the mess one has to deal with.

Weary and exhausted, Angelika walked over to the chainsaw, ready to finish this and get a nap in before Harold came home, but to her dismay, the chainsaw wouldn't start up.

"You've got to be kidding me! What's wrong with it? It's plugged in!"

And that was the precise moment when Harold opened the door and yelled, "Honey, I'm home."

"Shit," Angelika whispered.

Harold walked into the kitchen and froze.

"Honey, not on the tile. And is that our neighbor?"

* * *

Lexie's love of horror started early with the TV show Goosebumps and only grew from there. A strong voice for women in horror, Lexie has appeared at several conventions. She spoke in nine panels about women in horror and horror in general, even moderating one at RavenCon in 2019. She wrote fan-fiction to build her audience and reviews horror movies on weekdays on Twitter. Her two debut books, one of short stories, *A Fine Day for Murder*, and her poetry collection, *Into the Dark*, were published on Halloween.

The Raven Queen

by N.V. Devlin

The Raven Queen

By N.V. Devlin

Devlin crouched against the stone wall, ivy brushing against him. He hung his head between his knees, fingers clawing into his back as he sobbed. His heart beat a wild rhythm, trapped in its bone cage.

Thump thump thump.

If not for his ribs, that savage, pumping thing might have sprouted legs and run off into the woods ahead of him.

"Safe here." His gaze trailed after an ant crawling on the broken flagstones as he tried to control his trembling. He'd been made small, so very small, but now he was free. "*Safe safe safe.*"

Devlin's breathing slowed long enough for him to lift his eyes and survey his surroundings. Ivy climbed up to the vaulted roof, its roots digging into the stone's crevices. Those roots that couldn't worm into a crevice dangled from the ceiling.

Stained glass shards covered the floor while a wooden cross loomed over a stone altar and splintered pews. A church.

Devlin stared up at the nails hammered into the cross. "Faceless, mute." His pulse slowed. "Does anyone still worship you now that she's invaded our lands?"

No answer.

Devlin rose to his feet. "Did you see what she did to my sister? Or am I better off worshiping the wind?"

He waited for words. A whisper. A sigh. Any indicator that God had seen the abuses he'd suffered for the last many years when he'd traded his life for his sister. It had been a useless bargain, because Corvyna slaughtered her anyway, right before his eyes. Right before stuffing him into a cage.

A scream shrilled.

Devlin ducked down. His gaze darted around the ruins. "Please, not her."

Devlin rushed for the stone altar. He slid behind it and huddled close. He cursed himself for daring God, because if this was His answer, he regretted cracking open his lips.

Wings fluttered, and an icy blast blew through the abandoned church. Devlin's heart sputtered again, and he clasped his hands together as he mouthed his first prayer since becoming Corvyna's prisoner.

Please, he mouthed, *please hear me*. Frost veins jagged across the flagstones beneath his knees, stretching up to the cross. Ivy leaves shriveled and melted from the walls. *Lord, I am sorry for my earlier blasphemy...*

"He cannot hear you." Her voice glided through him like rain. "There are no gods. Only man and ravens."

Devlin glanced up, and he found Corvyna perched on the altar in her bird form, her talons piercing the stone. He gasped, words like icicle shards in his throat. His clasped hands shook, his body rooted to its spot.

"Hello, Devlin." Corvyna blinked fast, her black eyes reflecting his face, twisting with terror. "Did you think I wouldn't find you?"

"No." Devlin thawed from his fear and lurched back, dragging his body along the floor. "I ran so far. I *ran ran ran*."

"And I *flew flew flew*." Corvyna's mocking laugh seeped into him as she lifted her wings. Feathers whirled around her, detaching from her body, until she stood a woman, wearing a crown of glossy, ebony feathers and a black satin gown shimmering with bluish streaks. "You haven't finished your prison sentence."

"I did no wrong." Devlin's throat worked as Corvyna flicked out a hand, her talons growing thick and long in a flash. "M-My sister and I... We were hungry. I slaughtered them because I thought they were only birds."

"They were more than birds." Vengeance glittered

in her eyes. "They were my sisters, and you ate them like they were common fowl."

"I didn't know who they were…"

"You mean your *sister* didn't know?" Corvyna cackled as she glided towards him, her hem brushing along the ground. New veins of frost burst like lightning under each footstep. "At least I can credit you for sticking to your lie. I know it was she who caught them, slaughtered them, plucked them, and cooked them. It's why she died before you. And you ate them. It's why you will live in a cage for as long as it amuses me."

"Please," Devlin sobbed, hands raised to her in place of God. "Please forgive me, Corvyna. I've learned from my sins. I've spent years in that cage—"

"Where you will spend many more." Corvyna stopped before him, and bent down. She dug a talon into his chin, forcing his gaze to meet hers. "My throne room has been sullen without your wailing."

His Adam's apple bobbed. "Have mercy."

"Your sister had no mercy for mine." Corvyna sliced her talon into his chin. Warmth trickled down his neck, pooling in the hollow of his throat. "Freedom isn't for man, and it certainly isn't for *you*."

Corvyna snapped her fingers, and his cage materialized. Its rusted bars were wrapped with ivy, its door swinging wide open. She pulled a skeleton key from her gown. "Now get inside like a good boy."

"Never," Devlin shouted.

He vaulted to his feet and raced for the church's

entrance, its doors hanging on rusted hinges. Outside, it drizzled.

"Fool."

Cold winds blew with her voice. Before Devlin made it into the rain, black feathers whirred around him. He sucked in a breath of air, but instead of cursing her, screams tore from his throat as his bones cracked. Tears stung his eyes as ropes seemed to thread through his veins, squeezing, squeezing, until he shrank down to the size of a field mouse.

"Tiny human." Corvyna hovered over him before he could hide under one of the pews. She scooped him up and thrust him into the cage, locking him inside. "You've added more years to your sentence for daring to escape me."

He clung to the bars, crying, "Please."

"Oh, Devlin. My captive." Corvyna held up his cage, her onyx eyes glittering. "My sweet, sweet captive." She transformed back into a raven, spread her wings, and soared into the rainstorm with his cage dangling from her claws.

* * *

N.V. Devlin writes speculative fiction and psychological horror to better make sense of the world. N.V. was the 1st Runner-Up for Indecent Magazine's 2022 Queer Quivers Contest and has had work in the Creepy Podcast and Rebellion Lit's *The Start* anthology. Some favorite authors include Edgar Allan Poe,

Joseph Sheridan Le Fanu, Joyce Carol Oates, Shirley Jackson, and Neil Gaiman, and N.V. aspires to someday write even a fraction as well as them. Find N.V. on Instagram (@nvdevlin) for more.

UNARMED

by Warren
Benedetto

Unarmed

By Warren Benedetto

The amputation was the easy part.

It's incredible the kinds of things you can find online if you know where to look. I didn't even have to search for very long. I just put the word out through a few discussion boards of questionable repute, and a couple of hours later, I received a private message from a doctor willing to do the surgery, no questions asked. Even better, he was right in my city, just a short Metro ride away.

We met in a steam-soaked ramen shop the size of a shoebox, in an alley off Sixth Street. I wore a nondescript outfit: a plain black tank top and jeans, a pair of mirrored sunglasses, and a white baseball cap with an OI logo on it. I wanted to look as generic and unmemorable as possible. Just an average girl on an average day doing average things.

The doctor said he'd be alone at a table in the back corner of the shop. He was. I was surprised to see that he was relatively young, despite his thinning hair. He was dressed like you'd expect a doctor to dress, in khakis and a white-collared shirt with the sleeves rolled up to his elbows. He looked more like your typical Midwestern gynecologist than a black-market surgeon doing body modification.

As I approached, he slurped down a mouthful of ramen, then patted his lips with a napkin. I noticed a tiny four-dot pattern marked on the paper in black ink. It was a subtle signal that he was sympathetic to the Resistance.

His eyes momentarily flicked to the OI logo on my hat. I shook my head.

"Have a seat," he said, motioning to the empty chair across from him. I pulled it out and sat down. He spooned a mouthful of soggy pork into his mouth, speaking as he chewed. "Nice hat."

"If you can't beat 'em..." I said dryly, leaving the rest of the idiom unsaid. I took off the hat and tossed it on the table beside me. "You get the deposit?"

A few minutes earlier, I transferred five thousand coin worth of untraceable cryptocurrency to his account. The other five thousand were held in a digital smart contract that would be unlocked once I confirmed the surgery was done—if I survived, of course.

"Got it." He sipped his beer and put the bottle back down on the table. "So, which hand?"

"This one." I rested my left elbow on the table,

then drew an imaginary line with my right index finger around my left forearm, just below the wrist. "Around here."

"You're a righty, I hope?" he asked with a small grin.

"When can you do it?"

He shrugged. "Whenever you're ready."

"How about now?"

* * *

The recovery took about a month. I spent most of that time in my apartment, ordering takeout and doom-scrolling on the Internet. As usual, the news was a firehose of human misery. Just when I thought people couldn't be more immoral, selfish, and stupid, I was proven wrong by some new shock to the conscience, some new offense to basic decency.

The problems started at the top, with our Dear Leader. He was a detestable man, a malignant narcissist constructed entirely of human flaws, wrapped in a noisome, sweat-slicked rind, and topped with shoe-polish black hair that looked like a sea otter after an oil spill.

Just seeing his face flooded me with fury. He was the living embodiment of everything I hated, the antithesis of every value I held dear. His amorality was a contagion that infected the populace, injecting bitter poison into the nation's bloodstream until every heart seethed with rage.

Predictably, the hostility metastasized, escalating

from Internet feuds and shouting matches to fist-fights and firebombs. Misogyny, racism, and homophobia were weaponized, used as pretenses for further abrogating the rights of anyone who wasn't white, male, and Christian.

In the past year, ragtag OI militias had begun patrolling the streets, armed with automatic weapons and a cult-like devotion that bordered on religious. They sported the Dear Leader's insignia—a black circle with a red diagonal slash through the middle—on armbands and flags. It represented both the initials of his name—OI, Oliver Invern—as well as those of the Party's nationalistic slogan: "Original Intent".

It was a weirdly nonsensical phrase. Supposedly, it had something to do with defending the original intent of the Founding Fathers, but that was bullshit. What it really stood for was mayhem. Destruction. Chaos.

The descent into fascism was happening faster than anyone could have imagined, and the Dear Leader was accelerating that slide with every passing day. I never thought I'd see the day when firing squads were deployed in my own country, against my fellow citizens.

Journalists, scientists, doctors, and the like were being mowed down for the simple crime of telling the truth. There were no indictments. No trials. No juries. How could there be? The judges were the first against the wall.

The Dear Leader's depravity knew no bounds.

Someone had to stop him. A few months ago, I decided it would be me.

I would do it for the good of the country. For the good of humanity. And, most importantly, for my daughter.

Her murder destroyed me. I should have said something when her father—my ex-husband—started taking her to the Dear Leader's rallies, but I didn't. Instead, I convinced myself that she couldn't possibly believe the OI propaganda, that she would never dream of willingly following such a monstrous figure. But I was wrong.

The hateful rhetoric of the Dear Leader and his OI mob transformed her from a bright, kind, thoughtful fifteen-year-old girl into a sullen, angry teen who spent most of her time commiserating with other OI adherents about a litany of imagined injustices.

She became so enamored with the Dear Leader that her only request for her sixteenth birthday was a front row ticket to his upcoming rally, as if he was a goddamned rock star. Her father, of course, obliged. That night, the Dear Leader spotted her on the rope line after his speech and invited her to join him backstage for a special photo op.

She never came home.

Taking out the Dear Leader wouldn't be easy. I couldn't just waltz into a rally with a pulse rifle and expect to get anywhere close to him. His drones were everywhere. They had computer vision with advanced threat-detection algorithms that could identify a weapon from miles away. Explosives, too. The chemical signature from anything incendiary would light up their sensors like a Christmas tree.

I'd never considered using explosives anyway—I wouldn't want to risk innocent people getting killed. The same went for using any kind of firearm. A vehicle was out of the question—there would be no way to run the Dear Leader down without plowing through a crowd. Poison could work—in fact, it would be ideal—but that would require access, which I didn't have. I was a nobody.

No, if I was going to stop him, I would need to be more creative.

The human body had become a battleground, with a small minority of the population deciding what the rest of us could—or could not—do with our bodies. In a world of forced birth, gender reinforcement camps, race-based curfews, and other affronts to bodily autonomy, there was something delightfully subversive about my voluntary self-mutilation. It was more than just a means to an end; it was a statement unto itself.

I looked down at where my severed hand used to be. My stump was mostly healed. The surgeon had done an admirable job under the circumstances. The cutting laser quickly cauterized the wound, allowing it to heal with remarkable speed. It was easily the best amputation ever done in the basement of a ramen shop. But it was only the first step.

On my laptop, I opened the link to the doctor's crypto wallet. Typing with my one remaining hand, I entered the deposit amount for my next surgery: ten thousand coin. Then I clicked Send.

* * *

"I can't do that," the doctor said. He pushed his half-eaten bowl of ramen away. He looked nauseous.

"Can't? Or won't?" I asked.

"I mean, I could but... my God." He swallowed hard then grimaced. "Why would you want to?"

"No questions, remember?"

He nodded, then looked down at his hands. "Look, maybe you should find someone else. The extreme stuff isn't really my thing." He pushed his chair back and started to stand.

"Fifty thousand," I said.

The doctor paused, then sat back down. He leaned forward over the table. "Fifty thousand coin?" he asked in a hushed whisper. "Seriously?"

I nodded. He puffed out his cheeks and exhaled a gust of beer-tinged breath, then sat back and stared at the ceiling. His fingers drummed nervously on the table. He seemed to be thinking it over. Finally, he looked at me and spoke. His tone was grave. "There could be infections."

"I know."

"You could lose your whole arm. Hell, you could die."

"I'll take the risk."

"The pain will be unbearable. Even with the medbot—"

"I can handle it."

He crossed his arms over his chest and stared at me, shaking his head in disbelief. "Jesus. You're a sick fuck, you know that?"

"Is that a yes?"

* * *

He was right. The pain was unfathomable. I needed a double shot of nerve blocker from the medbot just to knock the agony down to the point where I could at least move my mutilated arm without vomiting.

The drugs dulled the pain, but they also dulled my senses, making me feel stupid and lethargic. That was fine for the last few days while I was trying to heal, but not for today. Today, I needed to be sharp. Alert. Ready.

Today, the Dear Leader was in town.

I stood in line outside the venue where he was due to appear and waited for my turn to pass through the security checkpoint. A fleet of drones buzzed overhead like angry wasps, scanning the crowd for threats.

Headless K9 quadrupeds patrolled the sidewalks like well-armed robotic dogs. The red lights on their side-mounted pulse rifles blinked steadily, letting people know their weapons were active.

I wasn't concerned. I blended in seamlessly with the Dear Leader's acolytes, sporting a cheap Chinese-made baseball cap unironically emblazoned with the nationalistic "I am a True Original" slogan and clutching a large Original Intent flag in my newly acquired prosthetic hand.

I laughed along as his supporters told sexist jokes and insulted a range of female politicians they thought should be punished by death. The fact that I was a woman didn't seem to bother them, as long as I signaled the appropriate virtues at the appropriate times. I mimicked the obsequious behaviors of a sufficiently cowed woman of faith, joining the show of hands to determine whether a disobedient wife should be punished by stoning, lynching, or both.

One of the supporters gleefully suggested that beating his beloved to death with a pulse rifle would be an acceptable alternative, but he was shut down by another, who reminded him that it would be a waste of a perfectly good pulse rifle. Laughter tore through the crowd; a good time was had by all.

Soon, it was my turn to pass through the check-point. As a bored-looking guard scanned my eye and compared it to the retinal signature on my ticket, I glimpsed my image on the security monitor.

The skin on my face was ashen, with a sickly sheen of sweat greasing my forehead. Dark circles pooled under my eyes like puddles of filthy dishwater. My cheeks were sunken smears of shadow. I looked like Death.

The guard handed back my ticket, then motioned for me to step into the full-body security scanner. I slid sideways into the cylindrical glass booth.

"Arms up," the guard intoned.

I followed his instructions, first raising my good

arm, then delicately lifting my prosthetic up next to my head. Whirling blades of agony tore through my amputated limb. I clenched my teeth and tried not to whimper. The machine hummed as it scanned my body from top to bottom.

"Step out," the guard said. He consulted the monitor in front of him. His eyebrows shot up. He looked at me, then at the monitor, then back at me again. "Secondary!" he called out.

Another security guard seemed to materialize out of nowhere. "Ma'am?" he said. "If you'll step over here, please?" He gestured to a screening area behind a large red curtain.

"Is everything okay?" I asked, with a careful mix of innocence and obliviousness. I stepped behind the curtain. He followed.

"Hands out, palms up." His tone was curt, very no-nonsense.

I followed his directions. My real hand was shaking, the fingers trembling like the tines of a vintage lie detector skittering across a roll of graph paper. It made the total stillness of the prosthetic all the more noticeable.

The guard eyed me warily as he scanned my body with a threat detector—a handheld version of the technology that equipped the drones. "You feeling okay?"

I choked out a short, bitter laugh. "Not really. Chemo sucks, you know?" The lie came easily.

The guard's expression softened a tiny bit. "Yeah, I hear you. Fuck cancer, right?" He glanced at the monitor, then at my hands. "Wow, okay," he said, nodding. "I see."

"What is it?" I asked, feigning ignorance.

He bent down and squinted at the display, furrowing his brow. He seemed to be trying to comprehend what he was looking at. "Your hand. The, uh..." He motioned awkwardly at my artificial limb.

"Prosthetic."

"Right. It's... it's showing up weird. Hmm."

"Well, at least you know I'm unarmed."

"Ha." The guard rolled his eyes at the pun. "Where's your husband?"

"Working."

"And he let you come here alone?" He cocked a skeptical eyebrow at me. The country wasn't quite at the point where women were barred from leaving the house without their husbands, but among the Dear Leader's followers, such limitations were common-place. The OI wives were willingly—even joyfully—complicit in their own oppression.

"He knows how much this means to me. I just—" I looked up at the giant portrait of the Dear Leader projected over the entrance to the rally, allowing myself to get choked up with emotion. "I love him so much, you know."

"He's a lucky man. Your husband, too." He gave me a sly wink. "All right, ma'am. You can go. Sorry for the trouble."

"No trouble at all." I flashed the Original Intent hand signal, making a circle with my thumb and middle finger and resting my index finger diagonally across it. "I'm a True Original," I said, parroting the customary greeting of the Dear Leader's followers.

"My Intent is pure," he responded in kind. Then he stepped aside so I could leave the screening area. "Have a good one."

I was in.

* * *

The rally was interminable, with almost two hours of bloviating by the Dear Leader before his tank of vitriol ran dry. In between hateful screeds, he announced his intention to expand the scope of his Fit For Service program to apply to all federal employees instead of just those in law enforcement.

It was positioned as a way to root out domestic terrorists from infiltrating the government. Really, it was a loyalty test designed to weed out anyone with "impure intent"—in other words, anyone who was less than one hundred percent faithful to the Dear Leader. Those who failed the test would find themselves banished to an Intent Center for "purification." Few would ever be seen again.

When the Dear Leader finally finished his diatribe, the applause from his devotees was like the roar of a jumbo jet, the kind of wildly enthusiastic response reserved only for hometown sports champions and fascist demagogues.

Waving to the crowd, the Dear Leader descended to the floor of the convention hall and approached the rope line, so-called because of the red velvet rope that separated him from the masses. Then he made his way along the line, shaking hands and basking in the adoration of his most worshipful fans.

The rope bumped against my thigh as I leaned over it to get a glimpse of him. He was moving in my direction. It was time.

With my good hand, I loosened the straps that fastened my prosthetic arm to my bicep. Nobody noticed as the silicone limb slid off and fell to the floor.

The Dear Leader drew near. He shook the hand of the man next to me, then turned his eyes to the man's teenage daughter. She was a slim, tanned blonde, maybe fifteen years old, whose womanly assets had already filled out her tight white halter top.

"Hello, my dear," he said. He took her hands in his. "Aren't you beautiful?"

I felt an indescribable wrath seething up inside me. I recognized that look. It was the same one he had given my daughter a year earlier, a few hours before her body was found, broken, used, and defiled, in an alley behind the hotel where he had been staying. It was the look of a predator eyeing its prey.

The girl didn't seem fazed. Of course not—she had no way of knowing what the look meant or where it might lead. Oblivious, she blushed and squealed as she captured the moment on her eyestream, broadcasting the experience directly from her retinal implant to her friends and followers watching online.

The Dear Leader gave her father a wink. "You're a lucky dad."

Those were his last words.

* * *

What happened next was forever memorialized in the eyestream being broadcast by Rebecca Vinton, the teenage girl who was next to me on the rope line. At the time of the incident, only a handful of Rebecca's friends were watching the stream.

Within hours, the Vinton Stream, as it would eventually be known, became the most-watched piece of media in the history of the world. It was like the Zapruder film, the 9/11 attacks, and the 2024 Portland massacre, all in one.

In the video, you can see the Dear Leader reaching out to shake my hand. You can see me grasping his hand in mine. At the same time, you can see my left arm thrust forward in what first appears to be a punch, just below the ribs. The arm draws back, then thrusts again. And again.

At this point, it becomes clear that I'm not punching.

I'm stabbing.

While this is happening, Rebecca is zooming her eyestream in on the Dear Leader's face, too absorbed in broadcasting the moment to recognize what's happening right in front of her. Her camera captures the Dear Leader's sudden recognition of the pain that is flaring through his torso.

Then it captures a blur of movement, a flash of white streaking through the frame. The Dear Leader's eyes go wide. They roll back in his head. Blood pours from his mouth and nose like a fountain. More seeps from his hairline and rolls down his forehead.

Most of what you see on the stream from that point forward is too chaotic to discern what's happening. But if you rewind to the moment when the camera zooms in, then you slow it down and play it back frame-by-frame, there are a couple of images that begin to tell a clearer story.

First, you'll see my left arm thrusting up into the frame, toward the Dear Leader, seeming to wield an unusual weapon. It's long, sharp, and grayish-white, like a thick plastic blade. A shiv, maybe, or some kind of fiberglass spear. You'll see the weapon plunging into the underside of the Dear Leader's jaw and exiting through the top of his skull in a spray of blood and brain matter.

Then, as the gore-drenched blade withdraws from his head, you might pause the video and look more closely. You might zoom in, focusing on my left arm, the one missing its amputated hand. You might ask yourself, how can an arm without a hand be holding a weapon? And then, at that moment, you might realize that the arm isn't holding a weapon. The arm *is* the weapon.

The weapon isn't a spear, or a shiv, or a blade.

It's a bone.

Two bones, actually, the forearm bones—the radius and the ulna—bonded together with resin and honed to a single knife-like point. Its skin and muscle are pared back and carved away, leaving twelve inches of sharpened bone protruding from an oozing, blood-caked stump.

It's the only kind of weapon that could have made it past the checkpoints, past the drones and the K9s, past the scanners and the threat detectors, past every form of security imaginable, to get within arm's reach of the Dear Leader.

As the Dear Leader's lifeless body drops to the ground, Rebecca's gaze spins away. There's some muffled audio—screaming mostly, as she is engulfed by the panicking crowd—then the recording abruptly ends.

However, if you pause it again, just a split second before it goes dark, you'll glimpse one final image as she turns: a ghostly face, with hollow cheeks and sunken eyes. My face.

I look like Death.

* * *

Of course, my face doesn't look much like that anymore.

After I slipped out of the rally in the ensuing stampede, I paid one more visit to the doctor at the ramen shop. He claimed he wasn't a plastic surgeon, so he couldn't guarantee a perfect result. But if I was willing to let him operate, he was willing to give it a try. He even volunteered to have his husband cut and dye my hair for me, to further disguise my appearance. No charge, of course, for any of it.

After all, I was a hero.

Walking out of the ramen shop that last time, I noticed something different about the city. It was quieter. The angry buzz of the drones was gone. There were no OI militias roaming the streets. The loudspeakers that had previously broadcast the Dear Leader's angry diatribes were silent.

A disabled K9 unit leaned broken and motionless against a pile of garbage by the curb. Its red lights were dim.

For the first time since my daughter's murder, I smiled. It was an unfamiliar feeling, especially with my new face, but I didn't mind.

I would get used to it.

* * *

Warren Benedetto holds a Master's in TV/Film Writing from USC. His early writing experience started in screenplays and TV scripts. After a 13-year hiatus, he picked up writing again in late 2019 and started writing short fiction. Since 2020, Warren's works have been accepted in about 150 publications. He writes dark fiction, mostly horror and sci-fi, or some combination thereof.

IN CROWD

by Rebecca
Cuthbert

In Crowd

By Rebecca Cuthbert

It seemed odd to Marge—a costume party? At their age? But George said no, not costumes—more like ceremonial garb, to ring in the new year. And hadn't she worn a choir robe each Sunday back at the Presbyterian Church in Boise?

Hadn't George worn his academic regalia at every U of I graduation, and would again, here at Seattle U? He was right, of course. And with the decade about to change over—1960!—what better time to try something different?

"Come on, honey," he said. "I want us to fit in."

She wanted that, too—to be invited to potlucks and the coupon club and the garden society. So Marge put on the dark, shapeless frock and half-length veil George had brought home, and he dressed to match—though he wore a robe with a zip front, not a gown, and a mask instead of a veil.

To complete her look, Marge painted her lips a deep shade of red and strapped on stiletto heels. If the party theme was "sexy mourner," she told herself, she'd be dead on.

* * *

At first, it was the usual small talk.

"How was the move?"

And "Are you settling in okay?"

And "Does George like the new job?"

Then compliments on the decor and the catered food and the heady red wine served by handsome young men in vests who kept the guests' glasses full. Cigar smoke and laughter.

Lively music, one record after another, spinning on the hi-fi. The only thing that made this party different from any other academia-crowd get-together Marge had attended with George over the years was the dress code: women shrouded in swaths of dark fabric, men in matching robes. Everywhere, obscured faces.

Marge was tipsy within the first hour. But the waiters kept filling her glass and her new friends told her to drink up, and since it was a party, she did.

After two hours, tipsiness gave way to a comfortable drunk. She laughed at bawdy jokes and smoked a cigarette someone offered. She even danced twice with Ed, the chair of George's department, who slid his hand up her dress to squeeze her bottom and sighed when Marge's hands returned the compliment.

Three hours in and approaching midnight, a pleasant warmth spread through Marge's body, loosening her limbs as she swayed with the music. Lights were turned down and glasses filled up and Marge swallowed more of the sweet, spicy wine.

A trickle leaked from the side of her mouth and fell onto her dress, disappearing into the black fabric. Then the music stopped, and the lights winked out.

Whispers in the dark. Heated bodies pressing in.

Marge wanted to find George, but didn't trust her feet to move. The room spun. She closed her eyes and opened them again when she felt someone slide behind her, put an arm around her waist and pull her close.

"George?" she whispered, half turning.

But "Shhh," Ed said into her ear, holding her tighter. "The fun's starting," he breathed. "Watch."

Candles flared, illuminating the coffee table in the center of the room. Party guests crowded in to form a loose circle. Music started, but not for dancing.

These notes were slow, twisting, and ran up against monotone chanting in a language Marge didn't recognize. Chanting and humming, too, humming that came from all around her and then, she realized, from her own chest.

More candles were lighted. Blurred faces flickered, teasing through the dark. George, there, across the circle, not alone. Holding onto someone, a blonde woman, the way Ed held onto Marge, moving behind

89

the blonde the way Ed moved behind her, and it felt nice.

Marge hoped George felt nice too, and she knew Ed felt nice from the way his chanting stuttered and hitched, and she knew the blonde felt nice from the way her mouth opened in an O and she stopped humming, so Marge hummed for her, louder and louder.

Next to George and the woman, two men writhed against one another. A partnerless woman kneeled in front of them and touched herself.

Then, pushed onto the coffee table—knocking candles over, making it harder to see—one of the waiters. No vest now, no shirt, dark material gagging his mouth with more binding his wrists.

His handsome face looked serene, though, not worried, so Marge didn't worry either, just reached back to clasp Ed's thigh and bend lower, her eyes moving from George and the blonde to the youth on the table, someone hoisting dark skirts to straddle his chest.

It was the hostess. Marge couldn't remember her name. Janine? Eileen? But then Ed moved faster and Marge closed her eyes, still humming, humming, and then Janine-or-Eileen called out:

"To the new decade!"

And Ed shuddered and Marge opened her eyes. Candlelight glinted off something metallic and there was so much blood. Someone caught it in a silver pitcher while others leapt forward, cupping their hands, lapping at their palms, voices yelling "Happy New Year!"

Ed pushed Marge toward them.

Then, again, a flood of darkness.

* * *

George tugged on Marge's hand, pulling her toward their sedan, parked down the block from the party. Her heels rang out on the sidewalk and she looked behind her to see other people in dark dresses getting into other parked cars, beeping and waving as they drove away.

"Time to go home?" she said to George, who was smiling.

"Not quite, love," he said and drew her close to kiss her hard, then helped her into the back seat, not the front, where he murmured into her neck, asking if she liked watching him and the blonde, if she liked the way Ed touched her, if she liked the ceremony's finale.

Marge looked at her hands, smeared dark in the streetlights' glow. She recalled the waiter's bare bleeding chest. Felt, again, the stir of desire.

She pushed George beneath her, leaned down and whispered:

"Yes, Yes, Yes."

* * *

Rebecca Cuthbert writes speculative, slipstream, and dark fiction and poetry. Her debut poetry collection, *In Memory of Exoskeletons* is out now from Alien Buddha Press, and her poem "No Rest Nor Relief For You With Me Dead" will be part of *Shakespeare Unleashed* (Monstrous Books and Crystal Lake Publishing). Additionally, her hybrid collection, *SELF-MADE MONSTERS* will be released in fall of 2024. For publications and more, visit rebeccacuthbert.com

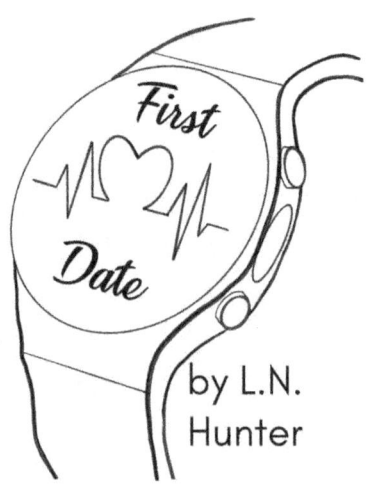

First Date

by L.N. Hunter

First Date

By L.N. Hunter

I watched one of those old movies the other day, from when nobody wore masks. It was a little disturbing to see all those strangers' naked mouths, and sometimes it was tricky to tell what was going on, since a lot of old-timey actors weren't very good at showing their emotions in their eyes.

Afterwards, I spent ages trying out different facial expressions in the bathroom mirror, trying to get my mouth to match what my eyes and eyebrows do naturally—it's hard!

I got a DM from Remy as I was doing it—my SomaNet had tripped an alarm because of my elevated heart rate and breathing, and signaled everyone I'd registered as my health watchers. That's Mum, my sister, best friend Joss, and—of course—Remy. The others probably didn't even notice, but

Remy overreacted, as usual—I guess it's kinda sweet that she worries so much.

I gave her a vidcall back, and she couldn't help but laugh when I explained what I'd been doing. It was weird how laughter in the movie differed from hers, as if the bottom halves of the actors' faces were somehow loose while their foreheads were unnaturally static.

Mind you, I did notice that Remy's mouth seemed a bit too rigid. I wondered if she'd joined in with that fad for botoxing your cheeks that a lot of the girls, and a few of the boys, at school were doing. It seemed rude to ask.

When she stopped laughing, she asked, "Still coming over tomorrow?"

I felt a sudden chill and wondered if she noticed *that* on SomaNet. I swallowed. "Sure, nothing can keep me away."

Her eyes smiled back at me, and I resisted the temptation to check her vitals on SomaNet to see if she was worried about the visit, too.

I couldn't stop thinking about the trip when I went to bed. It took ages to get to sleep, and I woke up feeling really groggy this morning.

It was my eighteenth birthday a couple of weeks ago, and we've talked about a real world visit every day since then. The confirmation email allowing me to travel unaccompanied finally turned up yesterday, so tonight's the night. We've been dating for about three years now, texting and video calls mainly. And some of those vidcalls were a bit... raunchy.

I'd made sure to take off my SomaNet band before we started, so that Mum and the others wouldn't see embarrassing vital stats readings. We even tried VR a couple of times, but it was always kinda awkward when Mum and Dad saw me grabbing the family kit, knowing full well that it would be Remy on the other end. Our VR set is a bit crap anyway, so it always felt like I was squeezing, and being squeezed by, some weird spongy toy when we "played".

Besides being nervous about meeting Remy with no screens between us, I have to admit I'm a bit scared to be outside on my own, not to mention traveling so far. Remy lives more than seventy miles away —that's going to take three hours on the train, what with the disinfectant protocols at the stations and county border processing.

Some families have their own private transport, but Dad says that's a waste of money. Like most people, he and Mum work from home, and school's totally remote-based, too.

There's no point in paying to maintain a car; and non-business fuel tax is astronomical, specifically to discourage traveling. We never go anywhere farther than walking distance—even then, we step outside the house at most once a month.

That's always a palaver: putting on the outerwear takes a good ten minutes, and my helmet *always* steams up. Oh, sure, some people just wear mouth coverings, but there are fewer health patrol stop-and-checks if your whole face is enclosed.

It's quite nice to be outside, seeing flowers and

trees and stuff, even if it is through a steamed-up mask, but it's always a relief to take all that gear off again.

I bought a new t-shirt for my visit. It says "I wanna touch your skin" on the front—I hope Remy doesn't think it's too rude; I certainly daren't let Mum see it!

Fortunately, the oversuit hides it when I get dressed to go out. My palms are sweaty, and the mask steams up even before I leave the house.

Mum looks ever so worried as I head to the airlock, but she'll be able to see exactly where I am all the time via SomaNet tracking, so there's really no need to worry. Today's viral load forecast is low to moderate, thanks to the stiff western breeze, so it's a fairly safe day to be out.

I wave to her through the airlock window, then set off. The outside world seems a lot bigger and emptier now that I'm on my own.

At the station, I scan my ID card at the ticket barrier and wait a tense dozen or so seconds while the machine checks my vaccine record and recent SomaNet stats. Finally, the automated voice says, "Proceed to Platform three, Embarkation Pod ten, Seat A," and the gate opens.

I swallow as I catch my first glimpse of Platform three—it's crowded! There must be a dozen people there, at least. A couple of the pods have families in them, but most contain a single traveller or no one at all.

I'm relieved to see that Pod ten is empty. It remains so, apart from me, until the station entrance closes, which means I'll have a seating block inside the carriage all to myself.

Someone in Pod five coughs. Everyone stares at them, but the cough isn't repeated.

The train doors open and I enter the carriage through a mist of disinfectant spray. My seat's still damp from the train's deep clean after the previous passengers disembarked.

I brought a book to read but end up staring out the window, watching the countryside and villages drift by. I can see some roads too, occupied by delivery lorry chains and the occasional car. We pass one of those traveller camps—refugees, Mum calls them—where people don't have masks or other protective gear.

I don't know if it's because they don't believe in the virus, even now, or if they simply can't afford protection. Maybe they're part of the one percent who are immune. I stare at the people standing around outside and wonder how many will die.

The train stops at the border, and an inspection robot rolls along the aisle, scanning ID cards and taking temperatures. There's an argument at the entrance to one of the family blocks farther down the carriage; it seems one of the kids is measuring hot, but it looks like they're getting away with it. I count my blessings that my block is far from that one.

Remy lives with her older sister in a flat not too far from the station. That's good news, because it means I can walk instead of having to take a taxi or other public transport.

I'm not so keen on the flat arrangement, though—shared stairs and corridor. I have no other option, though it does briefly cross my mind that a ladder to their window would be safer.

I spray my gloves and use an anti-viral wipe to touch the door handle, then make my way to her front door.

My heart's thudding. I know I'm going to have to take my suit off inside. What's it going to be like breathing the same air as someone who isn't family? A band tightens around my skull.

I'll be sitting on someone else's furniture and eating and drinking from things they've touched. My skin goes clammy, and I shiver, hands tightening into fists. What if Remy wants us to touch each other? I wish I wasn't wearing such a stupid t-shirt.

I feel dizzy as I stand at her door, and force myself to inhale and exhale slowly. Maybe I should give up and go home—that's the safe thing to do. We can talk on video.

I feel sick. I try to think of excuses I can give Remy when I get home. I wonder what my SomaNet is showing—it must be telling everyone I'm ill. Heat rushes to my face as I realize that it's also telling everyone on my network exactly where I am. Remy knows I'm here.

I reach out to the buzzer. No, I can't do it. I should just leave. Who needs a girlfriend, anyway? It's safer to be alone.

I turn round. I start to take a step away from the door.

Then I stop and close my eyes. I imagine Remy's face. My heart rate slows a little. I picture Remy on the other side of that door and its airlock. She might be as close as five paces away.

I open my eyes, turn round again, and press the buzzer.

* * *

L.N. Hunter's comic fantasy novel, *The Feather and the Lamp*, sits alongside works in anthologies such as *Soulmate Syndrome* and *Hidden Villains: Arise* as well as Short Édition's *Short Circuit* and the "Horrifying Tales of Wonder" podcast. There have also been papers in the IEEE *Transactions on Neural Networks*, which are probably somewhat less relevant and definitely less fun. When not writing, L.N. unwinds in a disorganised home in rural Cambridgeshire, UK, along with two cats and a soulmate.

GETTING
Personal

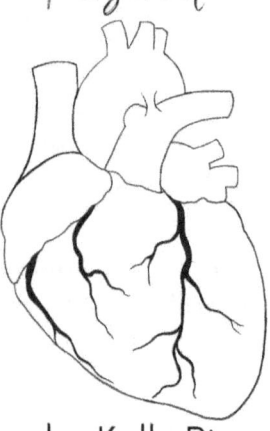

by Kelly Piner

Getting Personal

By Kelly Piner

She stood in her motel room and peered through the worn orange curtain, awaiting his arrival. When she had first received the alert on social media a couple of months earlier, her pulse had quickened. Could it really be the same Todd Wade?

Now Linda fluffed her hair and nervously double-checked her make-up in the bathroom mirror. After twenty years, she had to be dazzling.

Divorced for two years, Todd still resided in the same quaint college town where they had met and where he now worked as a research engineer. But after he had broken off their engagement, Linda had moved all around the country, working as a business consultant before she settled in the Midwest.

Her husband, Jim, had been killed in an auto accident last year, and she had neither dated nor socialized since. This trip symbolized a new beginning, a second chance at happiness, maybe even love.

A little after seven PM, a car door slammed and someone charged up the concrete steps. Not wanting to appear too eager, Linda waited a few seconds, following his knock before she answered. Her mind raced with questions. Would he look the same? Would she still find him attractive?

But when she opened the door, her stomach sank. Todd, now overweight and bald, looked sloppy in shorts and sandals. She wouldn't have recognized him had she passed him on the street. She felt foolish for dressing up in a black cocktail dress, but he had stressed how he would take her to one of the town's top restaurants.

He stepped inside the motel room and gave her a big bear hug.

"Let me look at you," he exclaimed, gripping her arms. "I can't believe it. I just can't believe." He sweated through his t-shirt and exuded an unpleasant, musty odor.

Linda pried herself free and laughed nervously. "Todd, it's been so long." That's all she could manage.

He took up too much space inside the small room, so she picked up her beaded clutch.

"I'm starving," she said. "Let's head out to dinner. We can talk on the way."

In the parking lot, Todd held his hand on the small of her back as they approached his car, an older compact with a rusted fender. The passenger door handle hung loose, so Todd had to pry it open from inside. Old fast food bags and soda cans cluttered the floor, and crumbs covered a section of the passenger seat.

She recoiled. It had been a stupid idea to come, and by the look of it, maybe she had been fortunate that he dumped her all those years ago.

Todd grabbed the bags off the floor and tossed them into the back and brushed some crumbs off the seat, apologizing all the time. When he settled and turned the key, it spit and sputtered.

"Excuse the car," he said. "I'm shopping around for a new one. You might want to lower your window. The AC went out last week."

Even at seven o'clock, temperatures in the small southern town still hovered in the mid-nineties, so Linda did as he said and lowered the window. Her hair clung to the back of her neck and perspiration dribbled inside her silk dress.

As they drove, the wind destroyed her carefully arranged curls, and she struggled to hear Todd over the roaring of the muffler. The drive to the restaurant felt like an eternity.

He wheeled through the crowded lot and parked on the curb two blocks from the restaurant. Inside The Country Barn, they joined a long line.

"Not to worry," Todd said. "I know the owners. Jack and Sharon have reserved us their best table. Nothing but the royal treatment." But when he approached the hostess, she shook her head and said they'd have to wait in line like everyone else.

Most of the patrons wore shorts and t-shirts, so

Linda felt over dressed and self-conscious as she tried to make small talk over the noise. And with no chairs available, her feet now throbbed from walking and standing in the new dress heels. Nearly forty-five minutes later, the hostess ushered them to a cramped table wedged between the kitchen and bathroom.

The continuous racket of slamming doors and clanking pans made conversation nearly impossible—not quite the romantic hideaway she had envisioned. She felt a little sorry for Todd, who had obviously put some thought into the evening, so she tried to be a good sport.

But awkward silences and feeble attempts at conversation made it obvious that twenty years was just too wide a gap to bridge. Todd mostly talked about his divorce and his fifteen-year-old daughter, Jamie.

And then tears filled his eyes. "I don't want to ruin our evening, but Jamie isn't doing well. She has kidney disease and needs a transplant."

Linda reached across the table and clutched his hand. The inconveniences of the past couple of hours now seemed trivial. He clearly adored his daughter, and so what if he didn't look like a movie star? She'd keep an open mind and not judge him too harshly.

After dinner, they visited their favorite old coffee shop at the edge of campus, and then Todd dropped Linda off at the motel a little after eleven. He gently kissed her cheek. "Thanks for understanding. It means so much having you back in my life."

In her room, Linda slumped onto the edge of the bed. She'd fantasized about champagne, dancing, and a walk in the moonlight. Instead, she had gotten a broken down old car and a hero forty pounds heavier.

Had she expected too much? Throughout their marriage, Jim had always reminded her of a suave movie star from the forties. But she didn't want to compare Todd to Jim. It wasn't fair.

Besides, tomorrow was a new day with new possibilities. She didn't like being alone. She and Jim hadn't had children, and she had no siblings. Her parents had died years ago. She couldn't afford to write Todd off so quickly.

* * *

When he arrived again the next morning, Todd looked drawn and preoccupied. He suggested a donut for breakfast on campus.

"Well, maybe not a donut—"

"I'm sorry. Of course not. But I'm no fun today. I want to tell you more about Jamie. Will you come back to my place? I'll make coffee."

Linda reached out and touched his arm. "Sure. I'd like to help if I can."

Todd lived in a rundown apartment complex, the kind of place where college students shared rooms. Sheets covered barren windows and loud music blasted from the parking lot where a group of teens had congregated.

Inside, his furniture looked worn and mismatched,

like castoffs from the Salvation Army. Linda couldn't understand why he lived this way. Surely, he made a good living as a research engineer, didn't he?

Todd didn't make coffee. Instead, he plunked down next to her on a threadbare sofa and stared at the floor, now visibly shaking.

"Todd, what's wrong?" She rubbed his back.

"I mentioned last night that Jamie needs a transplant. Everyone in the family has been tested, and no one was a match. The wait list is a couple of years, and she won't live that long."

His voice trembled when he spoke. He showed Linda a picture of a lovely teen with long red hair. Then he took Linda's hand in his and looked directly into her eyes.

"There's just no easy way to do this." He continued. "Would you consider being tested to see if you're a match? I know it's a lot to ask, but I don't know where else to turn. I'm desperate."

Linda felt her expression freeze. Had he just asked her to donate a kidney? "Is this why you asked me here?"

What a fool she'd been.

"Oh God, no. Please don't think that. I really wanted to see you again. You were always so loving and caring...." His voice trailed off, and he muffled a sob. "I've asked all my friends and just about anyone who I thought would be remotely receptive. If we continue to see each other, you have to know everything. I don't want to lie."

Linda shook her head. "I don't know, Todd. I just

don't know. Surgery. My kidney. It all sounds like so much."

"I fully understand. But if you decide to try, the preliminary tests are quick and non-invasive, just some simple blood tests." He stroked her hand just as he used to and squeezed a little. "The doctor could see you tomorrow morning for some labs, and it shouldn't take more than an hour. Then you could be on your way back home." He examined her face, his eyes watery and pleading.

Linda looked away.

"Hey, I'm sorry. I'm out of line." He lifted his hand from hers. "I feel like I've ruined your trip. Let's head back into town and do some sightseeing. I promise not to bring this up again."

Relieved, Linda stood. "I think that's best. Let's go back into town." She forced a smile, but she couldn't wait to leave on Monday. She should have known better, attempting to rekindle the flame after so many years.

The two rode in silence back to Campus Drive. She understood his desperation to save his child. He was still the same compassionate guy she'd fallen in love with a lifetime ago. If she had a daughter, she'd probably do the same. But still....

As if sensing her confusion, he said, "You're probably wondering why I'm living this way, a rundown apartment and broken-down car. Jamie's medical bills depleted all my savings, and I had to borrow money. Following the divorce, I let Carol and Jamie keep the condo, so I had to move. I'm trying to get back on my feet."

Linda reached over and took his hand. "Don't worry about it." After all, she thought, what difference did an apartment or car make? It was the person who counted.

They strolled through the university arboretum and then sat outside a trendy bistro for a decent lunch of greens with beets and goat cheese and a tangy orange dressing. By the end of the long lunch, all the earlier tension and awkwardness had evaporated. Linda felt Todd had really opened up to her.

No longer offended by his request, Linda saw only a dedicated father trying desperately to save his daughter. She paid for lunch, insisting that she wanted to treat him, and then they walked around the small lake, ending up on a bench near the water's edge. They had a heartfelt talk about their dreams for the future. Linda cried when she talked about losing Jim. She had few friends and worked from home, she confided.

Todd leaned in and kissed her, and Linda had to admit that she felt a renewed attraction to him. Suddenly, his extra pounds and balding head no longer mattered.

When she spoke, her voice cracked. "I'll go to the doctor with you tomorrow for the preliminary tests."

"Are you sure? You'll never know what this means to me." He drew her close and held her against his chest.

Linda had no reservations. She was no doctor, but

she knew enough about transplants to recognize that her odds of being a match for Jamie were slim to none. This was a good faith gesture. It gave Todd hope, and she could return home absolved of guilt.

Back at the motel, Linda invited Todd inside. They embraced again and talked more about old times and hopes for the future.

After a lingering kiss at the door, he said goodnight. "I'll see you at nine," he said.

Linda slept well. She'd reconnected to Todd and couldn't help but dream of a possible future together. Perhaps Jamie could be saved. He still had a good job as an engineer and could get back on his feet financially. He obviously still cared about her. She could see it in his eyes, and in the way he touched her.

The world had become such a cold, lonely place. Did she really want to spend the rest of her life meeting losers in coffee shops like so many others she'd heard about? At least with Todd, she knew what she was getting.

She felt a twinge of excitement when she spotted him in the parking lot a couple of minutes before nine. He greeted her with a big smile and a bouquet of daisies.

"Just follow me to the doctor's office. Can I buy you a coffee before you head home?"

"Absolutely." Linda daydreamed of her future on the drive over. Maybe she'd even become a step-mom to Jamie. She softened at the thought.

Ten miles outside town, the medical office was

situated in a rustic country setting with barns and horse farms. Linda could see why Todd had chosen this peaceful and picturesque practice for Jamie.

Dr. Franks greeted them. A middle-aged, affable man with a warm handshake, his manner instantly put Linda at ease. He explained the preliminary tests. "It's all pretty routine. Depending on the results, we may need some follow-up testing. Any questions?"

Linda shook her head. He escorted her into a room where he drew the blood samples himself, without the assistance of a nurse, and this personal touch helped her relax.

Still, she had never liked needles, and she felt woozy. So many vials of blood, she thought. She asked if she might lie down for a moment. She fought sleep, but felt herself slipping in and out of consciousness. At one point, she looked down at her body, as if she had left it altogether.

* * *

Dr. Franks could not have been more pleased with the results. "Linda's the perfect candidate," he told Todd. The doctor read aloud from a clipboard. "Caucasian female, age forty-two. All parts accounted for: Healthy heart, lungs, kidney, liver, and eyes."

He rolled a body covered by a white sheet into an air-conditioned room for disposal later, then he returned to his office to rejoin Todd. "There will be a nice reward in this for you," he said. "So many healthy body parts. People are willing to pay top dollar."

Todd grinned sheepishly. No one would look for Linda Mastro. She was all alone in the world.

The perfect candidate.

Poor Linda. So naïve. If only he had more trusting ex-fiancées. He could make a nice living doing this. The doctor guaranteed it.

* * *

Kelly Piner's love for the macabre and dark fiction began in childhood after she read her first Poe story. Since that time, she has immersed herself in Lovecraft, Richard Matheson, Ambrose Bierce and Rod Serling. Kelly's favorite ghost story is by Mark Twain. At age nine, she began writing short horror stories for friends. Kelly's stories typically fall within the dark fiction/weird genre.

The Salem Devil

by M. Blankenship

The Salem Devil

By M. Blankenship

Salem 1692

To my father,

You know with absolute certainty my soul lies with God, and I bestow those beliefs upon my family. I am the head of my house. Nothing exists under my roof without my consent or knowledge. The Devil does not live inside my home. The Devil did not reside in my wife and daughter.

The townspeople burned my beloved family at the stake. They made me watch the fire blacken their flesh. Their screams haunt my every waking moment, and I recall the horrible stench as the flames consumed their precious bodies. I called for the violence to cease. I cried out their innocence.

Nobody listened.

I have pondered for many days and nights. I have

asked myself if the Devil did not reside in my wife and daughter, but in my soul. Father, I know God wants me to forgive them, but I cannot. I am not willing to grant them forgiveness. They did not hear me as my world crumbled into ash. I will make them listen now.

No, I am not a wise man or a protector. I am vengeful, and I seek the blood of all involved. It will condemn my soul to the depths of Hell, but I am already living it.

Do not condone what I am going to do, for I know you are a godly man.

I will not pervert the family name. By the time this letter reaches your hand, the Thomas you knew will be dead, unable to bear the grief. I will be nameless in my hunt. Not a soul will know of my existence, for not even I can resist the temptation of the Devil's scheme.

I will not ask forgiveness. I only plead for your understanding.

With love,

Thomas

* * *

Thomas pushed the chair back and rose to his feet. His bloodshot eyes never left the letter lying flat on the rough wooden table. The ink had yet to dry, the black letters ominous yet comforting. He'd bared his heart onto the piece of paper. Every emotion he tried to bury deep within over the past few days had surfaced. For the first time since his family's murder, his mind was clear.

In the morning, he would send out the letter. The dry hay around the back for his cow would be perfect fuel to feed the fire that would overwhelm his home of eight years. A fitting end for the life of a man whose family was accused of witchcraft by the townspeople he once adored.

He packed a spare set of clothes into a burlap sack and tossed it next to the back door. The untied sack revealed the black hooded cloak resting on top of the set of clothes. He crouched and pulled at the rope handle on the floor. The wood raised, revealing the hidden compartment underneath. He grabbed the weapons wrapped in frayed pieces of cloth: a musket, pistol, sword, and a dagger.

His mind whirled, and he considered taking all of them before shaking his head. Settling for the pistol, sword, and dagger, Thomas returned the musket and closed the hatch. While the sword wouldn't be easy to conceal, it was best suited for close combat should he need it. The dagger would be his weapon of choice. The last resort would be the pistol, and Thomas hoped he wouldn't have to use it.

What he was planning was best done quietly. While the townspeople condoned the murder of supposed witches, they would condemn his retaliation. He understood people feared the claims, but his family was innocent. Their only crimes were being female and friends with the neighbors whom the town murdered nights before them.

While the townspeople were trying to close the gates of Hell, they'd unleashed the greatest form of destruction: a Devil wearing human skin. Thomas would accept that title without regret, for his heart no longer pumped for his own life.

Although he wanted the men to feel the pain he felt, Thomas could not bear to take such atrocious actions out upon the innocent women who bedded them or the children who didn't choose their birthright. No, he'd go to the source. He planned to send the men to face judgement before he crossed the threshold himself. Thomas would take the life of every man responsible.

His mind returned to the men who beat him into the dirt and restrained him as others dragged his family from his home; the men who'd grabbed his loved ones; those who he pleaded with to release from imprisonment and a death sentence; those who set the pyres alight; and the one who gave the order to do so.

Rage simmered beneath Thomas's skin. He imagined what it would feel like as the dagger penetrated the flesh of his enemies, how the warm blood would stain his hands and clothes, and what expression the men would have as they gasp for their final breath.

Thomas kept running through the list of targets in his mind, etching their faces into his memory throughout the night. When the first sign of dawn settled in the valley, he traveled the familiar road to the postmaster. The families who were up whispered as he passed them. Thomas ignored them as he delivered the letter and returned home.

A mixture of lantern oil and flame had the house alight within minutes after Thomas left through the back door, trekking into the woods with his weapons and burlap sack. The shouts from the townspeople reached the tree line, but he didn't spare a glance back as the last constant thing in his life turned to ash.

He chose the cave systems in the middle of the woods as his new home. Tall pine trees and sycamores shaded the area, and foliage provided cover from prying eyes. A small stream trickled down the mountain from the rain a few nights ago, and Thomas used the water to clean away the sweat from his brow.

Tonight, he thought. *Tonight, Mr. Hearns will die.*

The list he'd made weighed heavily in his pocket and served as a constant reminder of what he'd lost. He'd carry it with him until the end, without a shred of doubt festering within. Amid the birdsong through the woods and the distant chirps of squirrels, Thomas's heart twisted.

They would've loved it out here, he thought. *It would be beautiful if they were with me.*

He recalled his daughter's laughter as she watched squirrels leap from tree branch to tree branch. She'd try climbing after them, her fearless nature forgoing any sense of safety, before Thomas returned her to the ground. Rosalie would watch with a smile that melted his heart, her laughter piercing his soul as his love for her amplified. Family meant everything to Thomas.

Now, they are gone. Taken from me by those we trusted.

Bitterness and grief settled in his stomach even as he hunted for small animals and gathered berries. Bile burned his throat as the food threatened to come back up his neck, but Thomas forced it down. There was no time to grieve. He had to prepare for the task ahead.

As night descended in the woods, Thomas's eyes adjusted to the moonlight shining through the branches in the trees overhead. The campfire he had lit earlier faded out to nothing but embers as he held the dagger in his hands.

There is no going back after this.

He returned the dagger to its sheath and rose to his feet. The cloak provided warmth from the night air as he traveled through the woods and back to the town. A few twigs broke underfoot, but Thomas kept a constant pace. The moon moved until it was overhead. Little light from oil lamps shone through the town, most of its occupants buried under blankets and furs for the night.

But not Mr. Hearns.

For all his preaching about sin, the man spent a lot of time in taverns with many soiled doves and searched for the bottom of an ale bottle every night. His wife knew of his betrayals but remained silent to avoid being pummeled.

There were many times when Thomas's wife,

Rosalie, would open their door to a sobbing Mrs. Hearns. Thomas would go into a rage, only to be stopped by the abused wife's pleas for the violence to cease. The acts repeated. As long as Mrs. Hearns protested against punishment toward her husband, there was nothing that could be done.

Thomas found his target in front of the tavern, throwing back the last bit of ale left in his mug before tossing it into the dirt. The man wiped his mouth with a clothed forearm before stumbling down the street. Thomas followed through the darkness, trusting the dark cloak to conceal him from the eyes of any potential witnesses.

His long stride made Thomas catch up to the man within seconds. Heart hammering in his chest, Thomas drew the dagger from its sheathe.

"Father, forgive me," Thomas said, "for I shall sin."

Thomas's arm wrapped around Mr. Hearns' shoulders and chest. The man's slurred protest turned into a wet gurgle as the dagger sliced through his throat. Mr. Hearns fell to the ground like a puppet with the strings cut. Wide eyes stared up at Thomas.

"You helped take my loved ones from me," Thomas said. "You shall love or lust no longer."

With one last choking noise, Mr. Hearns's body became lifeless. Blood pulsed from his torn throat and spilled into the dirt. Thomas retreated into the woods, half-expecting the shouts or screams of witnesses to follow. None came.

Thomas took his time. While vengeance burned in his soul and awakened him every morning, he refused to die before his mission was complete. He remained in the woods for a week, not daring to venture into the town. When he finally did, he met another gruesome scene: a husband screaming as they hanged his wife for the crime of witchcraft.

By the time Thomas entered the crowd, she was dead. Her eyes bulged from their sockets. The once pink hue of thin lips was as purple as the rest of her face. Thomas tore his eyes away and focused on the grieving man, who had collapsed onto his knees.

As the crowd departed, Thomas followed their example and withdrew into a small alley. The grieving man remained in the dirt and stared at his dead wife until the sun set. He rose to his unsteady feet and moved down the street. Thomas followed him.

The man collapsed onto a porch and buried his face in his hands. Silent sobs wracked his body once again. Not seeing anyone near, Thomas moved to sit next to him.

"Please," the man said, his voice breaking. "Leave me be."

"I witnessed what happened. She did not deserve such treatment."

"Then why in God's name did they do it? What part of God's teachings tells us to murder people and justify it by accusing them of sin? My wife was innocent!" The man had risen to his feet and spat toward the gallows.

"No such thing exists in God's teachings," Thomas said. "I share your grief. Those men took my wife and daughter from me."

The man wiped away his tears with the sleeve of his shirt. "We moved here a few days ago, but we should've never left her parents' homestead."

"We cannot change the past, so I offer you a path of vengeance." Thomas stood and offered his hand. "Join me, and we will make them pay for their transgressions. We shall spill their blood."

Silence. As Thomas's hand lingered in the air for those few moments, he wondered if he'd chosen the wrong potential ally. The man looked at the ground. A wave of disappointment flooded through Thomas as he turned away.

"I understand my offer sounds sinister. I do not wish you any ill-will. This path isn't traveled by the weary. Forget our talk." He walked away, heading toward the woods again while his mind raced with plans. While getting the town to rebel would be easier than picking people off one-by-one, not everyone wronged shared the same mindset as him.

"Wait!" the man's voice called out and stopped Thomas in his tracks. "I am no killer, but I'll be your eyes in this town on one condition. If I inform you of a lynching or burning, stop it. No more innocent people shall die as long as we can prevent it."

"We?" Thomas turned to face the man. "I am the one dirtying my hands, boy."

"I am the one remaining in enemy territory," the man said. "They will put my head on a chopping block for my disloyalty. You seek my help. Those are my terms."

Thomas grinned. "You do not fear death. If you

did, you would not have spoken to me in such a manner. What is your name?"

"John."

Thomas nodded. "Should you have information for me, leave a candle lit in your home after the town has retired for the night. I cannot promise to save lives, but I swear I will do so if it is within my capabilities."

"I'll accept that," John said. "What do I call you?"

"I have no name."

John huffed a laugh. "Then I shall refer to you as a French term a trader told me months back. The rough translation is 'assassin.'"

"As good a name as any," Thomas said. "Keep your head down, John."

"Yes, sir."

Thomas watched the man return to his cabin before returning to the woods. The birdsong did little to soothe his nerves. Somehow, his identity remained intact.

While it was luck, Thomas believed it would run out eventually. Dragging the family name into his deeds was the last thing he desired, but it seemed inevitable if he wished to stop the murder of innocents.

He waited near the town until night had fallen before tracking Blake Davis to his home. The traitor had been the one to first stand between his family and Thomas as the men dragged them to their death.

Blake tried to convince Thomas that Satan possessed his wife and daughter. Thomas wasted precious seconds trying to reason with him. Those

124

few seconds wouldn't have made a difference in his family's fate, but it was the treachery that burned the most.

Now, he shall burn, Thomas thought. *For he is no longer my best friend.*

Blake had no family living in his home. His wife died of an illness months before, which he blamed on witchcraft once the accusations started spreading through Salem. The two could never bear a child. Sneaking into his cabin was mere child's play.

The man sat in the darkness next to the open window. A floorboard creaked under Thomas's foot, and Blake lunged upward.

"Who's there?" Blake asked.

Thomas darted forward. The dagger buried to the hilt in the man's stomach. A pained gasp rushed past Thomas's ear before he removed the dagger and allowed Blake to fall to his knees. Thomas grabbed several strands of the man's hair and forced Blake to look up at him.

"You once called me friend, yet you refused to listen to me before allowing them to take my family to their death," Thomas said. "I hate you for standing between me and them and believing such lies about my family. I commit your soul to the Hell you deserve."

"Thomas?" the man's strained voice reached his ears. "Please. No. I'm—"

Sharp steel sliced through his throat, cutting off anymore words as Thomas let Blake fall onto his side. Blood rumbled in the back of his throat and his limbs jerked sporadically until stopping altogether. Thomas stood in the silence for a few moments longer, making sure no sign of life remained before lighting a candle on the nearby nightstand.

He knocked it over onto the bed of furs, then left. Nobody sounded the alarm as Thomas returned to the woods. Finding a stream, he washed the blood from his hands and arms before changing into a spare set of clothes.

He was my best friend once. I thought I would have doubts, but there are none. Perhaps my soul is as dead as those I've condemned?

Whatever the answer, Thomas didn't linger on it. It didn't matter. He died the day they burned his family alive. Vengeance overwhelmed the normally easy-going man. There was nothing left of the Thomas people had known before.

Another target fell a few nights later.

Then another.

Killing became difficult as the town caught on to what was happening: someone was picking them off one-by-one. Men gathered up arms and torches and patrolled the streets through the night in shifts. They blamed witchcraft for releasing the wrath of the Devil upon Salem. Thomas scoffed at their ignorance.

They feel safe in the daylight, Thomas thought. *Their guard will be down, for they seek a creature of the night.*

Thomas felt exposed as he walked through the town underneath the midday sun, and he missed the cloak he usually wore. The old, worn clothes of the trader he'd bribed hung loose around his waist, only kept up by a small rope. His head itched from the straw hat as he shifted it for the second time within a few minutes.

People passed by him, not suspecting the dagger he had hidden underneath the clothing. The pyres loomed in the plaza. Women cried and screamed nearby with their hands bound as the public demanded their blood.

It's just as John said. Two women are to be killed today.

Thomas unloaded the merchant cart but kept his eyes on the scene. Unease twisted in his stomach. The knowledge that his mission would be more difficult than usual weighed on his shoulders like stones.

"Pa, why are they screaming?" a child asked as he walked by with his father.

"Their screams aren't human," the father said. "That's the devils inside 'em trying to get out."

Thomas dropped a box onto the ground and bent to pick it up. He bowed his head and tried to keep the unbridled rage hidden from any prying eyes. White knuckles gripped the wooden handles for a few heartbeats as the rage moved from boiling to a mere simmer.

Disgusting.

The screams grew shrill, and Thomas stood straight as a few men dragged them closer to the pyres. A crowd formed around the scene as angry voices spat insults. Thomas retrieved a match from his pocket and struck it against the rough wood of the cart.

He dropped the match underneath the blanket covering the hay-filled wagon and made his way into the crowd. His hands touched the shoulders of several people as he moved through them. Making his way to the front, Thomas watched as some people threw rocks at the crying women.

Blood and bruises spread across their porcelain skin. Their red eyes darted across the crowd, as if seeking any sympathetic gaze among them. Thomas moved to the side and walked until he was behind them.

John hovered near a building nearby with a bag over his shoulder, holding clothes for the women. While the plan was simple, the daylight made Thomas's skin crawl.

"Fire!" someone yelled. "A supply cart's on fire!"

Taking that as his cue, Thomas stalked forward while gently pushing his way through the crowd. The men holding the women dropped them into the dirt as the storekeeper yelled orders for the men to extinguish the flames to save the supplies. Thomas's dagger sliced across the storekeeper's neck, and the orders ceased as blood flowed across the man's hands. The same dagger sawed through the ropes binding the women.

Thomas pointed. "Go to that building. A man there will help you."

While the fire distracted the townspeople, the women ran to John. Thomas remained with the storekeeper, listening to him choke on his own blood. Thomas scowled at him. "May you never utter such heresy again."

The storekeeper may not have committed the murders, but he was the one to spread the rumor that his wife and daughter were spiritually unclean. His words condemned innocent people to death.

"It's the Salem Devil!"

Their stares burned his skin, and Thomas ran. Men yelled as they pursued him, but Thomas didn't dare look back as he weaved through the streets and bystanders.

A loud bang cut through the noise and Thomas jolted forward as fire raced down his arm. Biting back the pain, he clasped a hand over the bullet wound and kept moving. The tree line felt further away than it was as the angry yells grew closer.

A hand grabbed his injured arm and dragged him into a building. Thomas pulled away from his attacker before a man's hand pressed against his mouth. As his eyes adjusted to the dimly lit cabin, Thomas's struggle ceased. His body grew weak as his father pressed a finger against his lips in a gesture of silence.

The townsmen passed by the cabin, their yells never ceasing as they searched for the Salem Devil. The men moved away from the cabin before Thomas's father, Richard, released him.

"What are you doing here, Father?" Thomas whispered.

"I read your letter. I come with a warning."

Thomas raised an eyebrow. "What warning?"

"If you do not cease your work of the Devil, I'll put an end to it myself."

Thomas scoffed. "You should not have come here. I told you I knew what I was doing."

"As do I," Richard said. "No son of mine will murder anyone without consequence. If you repent now, you may not take your place with the Devil as quickly. Fail to do so, and I will give the Salem Devil up to the townspeople."

"You would not dare," Thomas said.

Richard's fist met his cheek, and Thomas fell onto the floor. A metallic taste seeped into his mouth as his teeth buried into his tongue. Richard's foot shoved him onto his back. A heavy weight settled on his stomach, and knees pinned him to the ground.

Hands wrapped around Thomas's neck, and Richard's fingers tightened. Thomas pulled at the hands choking him and kicked as black spots formed in his vision. Blood rushed to his head and air failed to enter his lungs.

No, Thomas thought. *I still have to kill the minister.*

He couldn't dislodge his father as Thomas's body grew weaker. His hands grasped at his father's wrists with a last effort. Richard smiled down at him.

"You asked for my understanding," Richard said. "I do, my son. Now, I plead for you to cease the killing. You are too young to meet such a fate, and I cannot fathom the thought of you in Hell."

A black curtain closed over Thomas's vision.

"Rest, my son."

* * *

Salem 1692

To my father,

You knew with absolute certainty my soul lay with the Devil, and our family did not condone those beliefs. You were the head of the house years before me. There was nothing that occurred under your roof without your consent or knowledge. The Devil did not live in your home, but you knew he resided in me after my wife's and daughter's death.

I believed you would kill me that day. When I awakened on the cabin floor with a blanket covering my body and wound dressed, I failed to fathom it. Why? After I collected myself and dressed in a stranger's clothes, I left the cabin. I searched for you. I found you dressed in the attire I took from the merchant. The minister stood over your lifeless body with a bloody sword.

I couldn't make a sound as the crowd cheered.

When others did not, you listened. You understood.

I lost my father that day, but you gave the towns-people the Salem Devil. My sins were not yours to bear.

I completed my mission despite your wishes, father. The husbands of the two women I saved joined the cause. More recruits appeared after them. We stood against the Church as one. The minister will not speak such heresy any longer, for his blood drained onto my hands.

I do not care about the family name, for I have no family left. All I have connecting me to Earth are those I trained to kill, a society of my choosing. The rebellion is growing. More are opening their eyes to the wickedness in Salem and other towns. John said we are the start of the assassins in this part of the world.

The Salem Devil lives, even though I failed my family.

I shall take my place at the Devil's table soon, for I could not resist his scheme.

I will not ask for your understanding. I only beg for your forgiveness.

With Love,

Thomas

* * *

M. Blankenship has been writing since childhood but recently began to pursue the possibility of self-publishing or traditionally publishing her work. She wanted to connect to people and bring them closer by using characters they can relate to. The journey has been difficult, but she wouldn't change it. The people she has met and their advice to help her grow has been priceless throughout the years.

The Taste Of Water

by Ichabod Ebenezer

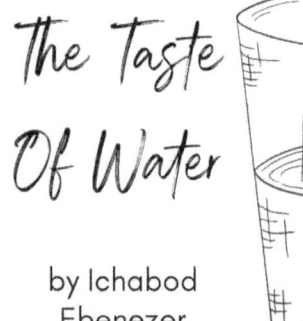

The Taste of Water

By Ichabod Ebenezer

I'm not in a position to tell you how any of this is going to end. I'm not a doctor or a scientist. I never even went to college. But if it's ever of use to anyone to know how it started, I was there. I saw everything.

My brother had a long weekend from college and asked if he could crash on my couch for a few days. He'd always wanted to see New York and was proud of my new job copy editing at the magazine. Of course, he wanted to celebrate, and to him, that meant more than beers, pizza, and Hulu.

"Come on. We're in New York. I want to move. I want to form tight bonds with people I'll never see again. I want to be surrounded by life, you know? Or else, what's the point in the big city?"

"My job is here?" I said.

James laughed. "Come on, Will, you work from home."

"I still have to go in for meetings sometimes."

"Whatever. Don't make me do this alone. I don't want to trust the Yelp rating. I want somewhere you've been, somewhere you know I'll like. Somewhere where there's lots of people who are there to have a good time."

"And you want me to go with you."

"Yes! I want to spend time with my brother. Come on, you never go out. Don't you sometimes just want to soak in a bath of humanity enjoying life?"

That was the difference between us. He felt this flow of endorphins from everyone around, jazzed up and partying. I only feel the people encroaching on my personal space, dragging me into conversations I have zero interest in, and God forbid, making me dance. "No."

"Well, too bad, because tonight we're going out, and you're sitting at the popular kid's table."

I ended up taking him to The Woods in Williamsburg. I only knew it for the taco truck on the patio out back, but my coworkers hung out there. It was trendy, there was a floor for dancing, and it was a short cab ride from my apartment in Bushwick.

Getting out of the cab though, it felt like a mistake. There weren't any lines yet, but I could see in through the front windows, and it just looked like a fire hazard with people packed in elbow to elbow. I never imagined a Thursday night would be so bad.

James turned toward me with a broad grin and

plowed in through the open door before I could say anything. Oh well. I could survive one night if it made him that happy. That was the idea, anyway.

I caught up with James at the bar. He ordered a bottle of 'cerveza', and turned to scope out the room, leaning with his elbows on the bar. I ordered my stand-by, rum and Coke.

Moments later, this dark-haired lovely ducked through the crowd and emerged just between James and me.

"Desculpe-me," she said, flashing a contagious smile at each of us, and tapped on the bar with her credit card.

She wore a shifty, shiny gold top, and a short skirt. Her dark skin glistened, and she never stopped dancing. Tap, shuffle, tap, shuffle. All within that one-square-foot each of us had available.

The bartender came over, and the girl said, "Another green one, por favor." The bartender smiled and left, apparently knowing what she meant.

My brother made his move. "I love your accent. Are you from Mexico?"

I don't know if he was out of practice, or just not paying attention, but it was a crappy move, so I jumped in. "You'll have to excuse my brother. He's a bit of a heathen. That was Portuguese. This beautiful young lady is from Brazil."

"Oh, my, very good! I'm from Rio De Janeiro." She smiled at me again. It's amazing how some people's expressions can change how you feel. I'm not saying I was in love, or that I was suddenly comfortable in the crowded bar, but her contagious happiness almost made me laugh. Her smile, so genuine and open, said life was always good, and she'd never been hurt.

"Rio, huh? What brings you to New York?" my brother asked.

The bartender brought her a shot of Midori and a bottle of water, which he traded for her credit card.

"Obrigada." She quickly downed the shot. "I'm on holiday, with friends. I've been here all week, and I have to leave tomorrow, so I'm living the most I can today."

"I wish I'd met you days ago. I could have shown you around," my brother lied. He didn't know Bronx from Battery.

"I wish too," she said, unscrewing the cap on her water bottle. "I was so sick, though. I couldn't leave the hostel for three days. It wasn't fun."

"Well, I'm glad you're feeling better." James raised his glass.

She knocked it with her water bottle, then turned toward me, raising the bottle. I clinked it with my glass, already feeling like a third wheel.

"I woke up this morning feeling incrível." I had no idea what the word meant, but she made a fist and flexed her arms. Healthy. Hearty. Strong. "I had to make up for all my lost time. I want to laugh. I want to dance. I want to know what American boys taste like."

Both my brother and I stood up a little straighter. She laughed, musically, and drank deeply from her bottle.

She set it down and put a hand on each of our arms. "Do you dance?" she asked.

"My brother here does," I said with a smile.

His eyes said thank you for him.

The girl scribbled on the bottom of her bill and stuffed her credit card into her waistband. Then she pulled James onto the dance floor. I turned to watch them, sipping on my drink.

I was glad for him. Here was exactly how he wanted to spend his break. Though she was gorgeous, and exciting, and exotic, and tempting, I wasn't going to compete with James. This was his weekend. I watched them dance for a few moments, then the crowd filled in around them and I turned back toward the bar and my rum and Coke.

The music screeched and thumped. My inner ear followed every beat with a tiny hiss of its own that felt like cilia actively dying. It was hard to believe this was fun for anyone, much less the majority of humanity.

The spots James and the girl left—it only occurred to me now that I had no idea what her name was— were quickly filled in, and the man next to me slid his elbow farther and farther in front of me to make room for his buddies. I picked up my drink and reached between them for James's beer bottle, and stepped away.

The dance floor was a navigational nightmare of colliding bodies, oblivious to everything around them. A pickpocket could have made a fortune in a few minutes.

The patio out back was equally off-limits, with the

lines to the bathroom filling up all the space in that direction. I looked for a television, anything to divert my attention while I finished my drink. There was nothing. I started bobbing to the beat just to not look stupid standing there by myself.

"Come dance with us." A pair of lithe arms snaked around my waist. I turned to find the girl smiling up at me. Her scent was earthy and primal, and not a bit unwelcome. The thought of waking to that lingering flavor on my bed sheets was intoxicating.

I looked past her and locked eyes with my brother standing at the edge of the dance floor. He raised his eyebrows and motioned with his head, encouraging me.

"No, thank you. I don't dance." I said.

"Well, come on. I'll teach you."

"No, I mean, I don't enjoy dancing."

She leaned forward and tugged at my earlobe with her teeth. "I promise you will enjoy it with me." She slowly slid downward, swaying her hips as she went. Every part of me responded to this invitation.

For the barest moment, I let go and imagined myself on the dance floor with her, following her motions, trading off with James, fitting in with everyone around me, losing my train of thought and living in the moment.

Then I thought of after. She showed every sign that she intended to go home with one of us, maybe both of us, and that way led to more nightmares.

"You go ahead. I'm just going to watch."

She made a face suggesting it was my loss, then

turned and danced back over to James. The two quickly disappeared into the crowd.

I sucked my drink down in several quick gulps. Still, my throat felt like sandpaper. Man, if she had a sister who frequented chess clubs...

The discomforts of the room quickly asserted themselves over my thoughts. People pushed past on their way between bar and dance floor, nearly knocking my glass from my hand.

A mix of bad colognes and foreign sweat invaded my nostrils. The music went into a shrill crescendo for what felt like an eternity before dropping to a bass line accompanied by the entire dance floor jumping at once. The ground beneath me moved, probably only slightly, but it felt like I was falling.

I had to get out. The very room was trying to expel me, like a cancerous growth.

I caught sight of James and the girl. She had her arms around his neck and their eyes were locked.

They would be fine. I could make my escape, and their day would only get better. James could Uber back to my place, and if he truly needed me, he had his phone on him.

I returned to the bar, squeezing between people to set my empty down, then I swam upstream to get out past the bouncer.

"You can't take that outside."

I looked down, realizing I still had James's beer. I handed it to the bouncer and stepped outside.

The autumn night air was cool and sweet in my lungs. A breeze lifted the sweat, some of it mine, some not, from my exposed skin. The bass line that had evicted coherent thought, dimmed quickly to background levels, and the sounds of traffic on the nearby bridge signaled my return to the normal world. The pressure in my head slowly relaxed. I took one last look in through the windows and stopped.

People were backing away from the center of the dance floor. Several people had their phones out, aimed at James and the girl. James was standing, mouth agape, fear and shock in his eyes. The girl was still dancing, but doing an odd move involving a deep back-bend. Then I saw her face, contorted. Her eyes bulged, her mouth stretched to its limits, her jaw set at a painful angle.

"Something's wro—"

Before I could finish my thought, the girl disappeared in a blast of blood and chunks of flesh. A gray cloud followed, billowing outward to quickly fill the room and cover the windows in fine dust.

Panic set in, and a human flood poured out the door. People fell to the ground and were quickly trampled. Screams filled the air, and I just stood there.

The last thing I saw before dust obscured everything was James covered in gore.

"Call 911," I whispered.

The sound of my own voice broke me of my paralysis. I ran to the door, but the tide of bodies rushing to escape pushed me back.

"Call 911!" I said again, to no one in particular.

I pulled people off the sidewalk and out from under trampling feet. I wish I could say it was some

142

humanitarian gesture, but I was just trying to get to James. The doorframe bulged with the press of escapees. I tugged on arms to break up the blockage.

People spilled out and ran in all directions. They were all covered in this same gray silt. The sight brought back flashes from all those old videos of the towers collapsing.

I held onto one arm, and when the girl turned to face me, I yelled, "Call 911!"

She nodded at me, though her jittery motions and wide eyes betrayed the shock she was in. I returned to pulling people free of the jam. More bodies filled it in. I couldn't even see individuals. It was just one solid, fleshy object of screams and reaching limbs. I reached in and pulled. Hands clung desperately to me, and I pulled. Over and over again, I wrenched people out and more filled the gap.

As I clutched one flailing arm, my hand slid out of its grip and came away covered in blood. I reached back in with both my arms, but lost it among all the reaching limbs. I pulled and pulled, and suddenly, out poured James. He was alive.

I dragged him away from the spillway. Someone else could help the rest. James coughed and retched. We made it to the curb, and he collapsed, vomiting into the gutter.

That same gray dust was plastered to the blood and sweat that covered his body. I pulled my shirt up to cover my nose, only then realizing my hands were covered in the same mixture of blood and dust.

James coughed up the last of his stomach

contents. He stood, looking for a clean spot on either arm that he could wipe his face with, but there were none. Blood and bits of flesh covered him from head to toe.

"What the hell happened?" I asked.

He shook his head instead of answering. His brow was creased with shock and questions of his own. He had no idea.

"We need to get you to a hospital."

"No!" His response was immediate and certain, and came as a complete surprise to me.

"Why the hell not?"

"Look at me! They're going to think I did it."

"Did what?"

"I don't know. There must have been a bomb... In her purse? Behind her...? Inside her? Maybe the bartender slipped her something? Doesn't matter. I'm the one covered in... her."

"What are you suggesting? That we flee the scene? That we burn the clothes, destroy the evidence?"

"Dude, everybody is fleeing the scene. Look around you. I'm not going to hang around here waiting to get arrested."

"Okay, but no cab is going to stop for you, and we can't walk twenty-two blocks in New York without people noticing."

James started unbuttoning his shirt. "Give me your shirt."

"What? No!"

"What's going to attract more attention? Two guys

walking around shirtless in October, or one of them covered in blood?"

"The blood isn't even the most disturbing part." I could by then make out chunks of bone, strands of hair plastered to his skin.

James whipped off his shirt and balled it up. "I need your shirt to wipe myself down. Clean my face a bit so I can pass."

I started unbuttoning my own shirt. "I like this shirt," I mumbled.

We managed. He transferred most of the blood and gore from his face onto my shirt, then turned it inside out and bundled his shirt inside it. We walked back to my apartment, passing by several groups of people, and hearing sirens all around us, but no one challenged us.

James went straight to my shower, taking the clothes in with him. I turned on the news, trying to distract myself from the thought of my drain clogging with the remains of a beautiful Brazilian girl.

The bar did get coverage in the night's news rotation, but so far, they were calling it "a disturbance at a popular local club." Police were at the scene, trying to piece together what led to the panic. Witnesses claim there was an explosion, but whether this was a prank in poor judgement or something more serious was yet to be determined.

By the morning, it was the main story. They called it a terrorist attack, and the news crews parked nearby showed footage of people in CDC branded hazmat suits going in and out. They were working to determine whether anthrax may have been dispersed and were asking anyone who may have been exposed to contact the number on the screen.

My blood felt like it drained from my body, and I had to sit to keep from falling over. Anthrax.

"Hey, James!" I called. If it was anthrax, he got it full in the face, breathed it in for... how long did I spend clearing the doorway? Several minutes, probably. There could be no argument now. I had to get him to a hospital.

James didn't respond. After his shower, he collapsed on my bed, and I let him have it. I bleached and Drain-o'ed my shower like I was detailing a car, then took the couch.

Now, I pushed the bedroom door open a crack and called out again. "James?"

No response. My blackout curtains were drawn, and the only other light sources in the room were my bedside lamp and the dull red glow of my alarm clock. I pushed open the door to let in the light from the kitchen.

"Turn it off!" James yelled. Sheets shifted and the vague shape of a pillow flopped over in the darkness. Good. At least he was alive.

I stepped inside and closed the door behind me, wondering if I should be breathing in the air he was exhaling.

"James, they're saying it was a terrorist attack. That it may have been anthrax. We've got to get you checked out."

"No hospitals," he said, his voice muffled by a pillow.

"Are you not getting it? Anthrax, James. You could die."

"I feel fine."

"Oh yeah? Then why the blackout curtains?"

"The sunlight hurts my—" He stopped, swallowed, started again. "I didn't sleep."

Of course, he didn't sleep. I'm amazed I got any.

"Still. We should get you checked out." He moaned like he was going to argue, but I continued, raising my voice. "You're clean now. Any DNA that was on you is down my drain and bleached to oblivion. I hid last night's clothes. There's no reason to connect you to the girl's death."

Except there was.

While news crews and the CDC weren't talking about the girl, TikTok had gone viral with several videos of her dancing oddly, then just gone. At least one I found clearly showed James in the moments before the explosion, at ground zero, when the cloud of dust filled the screen a moment later.

"No hospitals. I'm fine. I just need some rest."

I hesitated. Was I going to report my brother against his will? What was the alternative? Let him die lying in my bed when I could have done something?

"Let me feel your head."

The blankets came down. "Okay, *Mom*."

His forehead was clammy, but it wasn't hot. "Fine.

But you call me if you start feeling worse. It's still a workday for me. I'll be right out there."

"Thanks, mom."

I let him be and tried to turn my attention to work. I had forty-three unread emails, I was late for a Zoom meeting, and I hadn't even had coffee. After pulling a can of Doubleshot from my fridge, I jumped on the call.

My mind drifted, and I had trouble focusing on the client needs until I pulled up another tab and looked up the early symptoms of anthrax exposure. Vomiting, check. Loss of appetite? Maybe. He didn't eat anything since showing up yesterday. Fever. Not so much.

I looked through the rest of the document for "sensitivity to light," but it never came up.

With that out of the way, I was better able to concentrate on work. I poked my head back into the bedroom during my lunch break, but it seemed like James was sleeping. I stuck around long enough to be sure he was still breathing and let him be.

After work, I was more forceful. I knocked to announce myself, then stepped inside. "Come on, James. You slept through the entire day. I'm worried about you."

James propped himself up on his elbows. "What time is it?" His voice sounded husky.

"Just after six. Let me feel your head. And don't call me mom again. It's getting old."

"Geez, fine." He sat up a little further and started

coughing. I held my breath, thinking back to the Covid days. *Should I be wearing a mask?*

His head felt fine. Not clammy like before, and definitely not hot. "How are you feeling? Are you hungry? You haven't eaten since yesterday."

"I could eat. I don't know. A little stiff? Still tired though, and really thirsty. What do you have?"

"I have DoorDash."

We had pho and spring rolls and watched the news some more. The attack at The Woods was still getting a lot of play. A White House spokesperson said it was not an anthrax attack, but that anyone who was there should come forward and get tested.

"Get locked away and disappear is more like it," James said in his gravelly new voice.

"When did you get so paranoid?"

He didn't respond.

Channel seven had some 'exclusive' footage from a viewer's cell phone. They blurred out the gory bits, but warned us of its graphic nature before playing it.

The Brazilian girl was already convulsing when the video started, and moments later, she pixelated, and a gray cloud filled the view. As the image jerked around, James's face came into view, stunned and covered in blood. The person filming ran past James, showing all the customers screaming for the lone exit, then turned back.

The dust cloud was already settling around James, still motionless, but where the girl had been, there stood a white, vaguely phallic tower, perhaps five feet tall.

The segment ended with a still frame of James's face. "Authorities are looking for this man. If you know who he is or have seen him, please contact the police. If you wish to do so anonymously, the number is on the screen."

"When did I get so paranoid? How about, it's not paranoia if they're really out to get you? God, I feel like it's still on me."

He left his half-eaten soup and took another shower, after which he went to the bedroom and I didn't see him again.

James coughed a ton in his sleep. At one point, it sounded like he horked up something nasty, but when I went to check on him, he was sleeping. I was so worried about him, but at least I knew it wasn't anthrax.

I was woken the next morning by a pounding at the door. It took me a moment to register that it was my door and not someone down the hall, and the knocking came again. I answered in my boxers and tank top.

"William Mayfield?" an Asian woman asked. She was in a lab coat and a mask and held what looked like a fishing tackle box. Behind her were two uniformed police officers.

"That's me. What is this about?"

"A witness said they saw you at The Woods the night before last, but you haven't come forward for testing. May we come in?"

A cold sweat prickled my skin. "I left before... whatever... happened. I didn't think I had to."

"It's still a good idea to test you in case you were exposed earlier in the evening. I'll just need a couple small vials of blood. Five minutes, tops."

"Sure." I stepped out of the way and directed her toward the kitchen. The cops pushed in behind her. I pretended I didn't care.

Were they here because of James? Did they know I had a brother, and if so, did they compare his picture to the one from the night club video? I glanced at the bedroom door, closed.

James clearly needed medical attention. Part of me wanted to give him up and hope he would forgive me someday. The news report didn't say what they wanted him for. Maybe they just want to know what he saw since he was so close.

The doctor set up on my table, opening the tackle box to reveal an array of medical equipment. She pulled out a rubber strap, a syringe, and two vials. From a different section, she pulled out a card, affixed a sticker to it, and slid it over to me with space for my contact details. She ran a thermometer over my forehead while I filled it out.

"How have you been feeling since that night?" she asked. "Any cough, sore throat, fever, stiffness in your neck, or trouble breathing?"

"Wait, I thought they said it wasn't anthrax."

"It's not, but we're still working to determine what it was," she said.

"Just answer the question," one of the cops said. A White guy with a Freddy Kruger tattoo poking out beneath his sleeve.

James and all his symptoms came to mind. He definitely had a cough, and he'd mentioned stiffness, but no fever. "No. None of that."

Then came the jab and a moment later, she'd filled the two vials. She tilted them back and forth before setting them in a slotted tray inside the tackle box. She taped a cotton swab to the crook of my elbow and folded my arm up.

"Thank you for your cooperation. You can remove that in one hour." She pulled the vials back out and slapped a sticker on each, showing me the numbers matched the one on the card. Then she returned everything to the tackle box.

"Wait, how soon will you know if I have... whatever?"

"As soon as we know anything, we'll contact you at the number you provided on the form. We're still not sure what we're looking for, so please be patient."

I still had questions, but she was heading for the door.

"Mr. Mayfield, do you live alone?" the other cop asked. This one was middle-aged, chubby, and Black, with a mustache.

"What? Yes. Why?"

"And where does that door lead?"

The bathroom door was open and easily recognized. The only other door in that direction was the bedroom. "That's my bedroom. I still don't get why—"

He nodded toward the living room behind me. "You have a bed, but your couch is made up for sleeping. Was there anyone else with you at The Woods Thursday night?"

"No. It was just me. And I wasn't there long." I swallowed.

The cops' eyes said the couch still needed explaining.

"I coordinate with foreign translators. Sometimes I have to work at odd hours. I make up the couch so I don't miss notifications." All that was true and hopefully read that way.

"Mr. Mayfield, do you know this woman?" the other cop asked. He held up a phone with a picture of the Brazilian girl. It was a still frame from one of the videos that had circulated before TikTok took them down.

"Yes. I saw her that night, at the bar. She said she was from Rio, but I didn't catch her name."

"How about this one?" He swiped at his phone and held it up again. This time, it was James. They'd managed to find a still frame from a video before he was covered in blood. My mind went to the bundle of bloody clothes in the garbage can three feet away.

"No. I don't remember seeing him." There I'd done it. Bald-face lied to the cops. Well, I couldn't tell them, "Oh yeah, that's my brother James. He's in the next room." I'd already been evasive about that. But now I'd gone and lied, and looming like the specter of death was the certainty that they would find out. Sooner or later, they would track that photo back to James, and they'd know.

If he started coughing now...

My fingers shook, and I balled my fist to hide them. Then I realized that was an obvious tell and rubbed at my arm like the blood draw was bothering me. God, I sucked at lying.

"Alright, well, if you do remember anything, give us a call." It was the Black cop again, and he was holding out a business card. I took it and thanked my stars.

James emerged an hour after they left. He went immediately to the bathroom, but I intercepted him on his way out.

"How'd you sleep?"

He approached the couch, pulling his head to one side. "I must have slept weird because my neck is crazy stiff." His voice sounded even worse, like he'd been gargling with a wire brush. "I had the most amazing dream, though. I was super famous, surrounded by fans and flashbulbs, and I was rushing to my limo, signing autographs, a girl on each arm... It was awesome."

"I'll tell you what. It wasn't for your singing voice."

That got a chuckle out of him. "Do me a favor, draw the shades, will you? And do you have any Advil?" He stretched his neck the other way.

"Sure," I said, pulling the blinds. So, he was still sensitive to light. "Far left cabinet, next to the coffee filters. When you're done, I ran across a video you should see."

He filled a glass with tap water, which I would have warned him against if I'd been paying attention. "Blech," he said after swallowing his pills.

154

"Sorry, bro. City water is the price you pay."

He poured the rest of the water in the sink and joined me at the couch. I brought up the video I'd mentioned. "Content warning. This is pretty sick."

I hit play.

The video started with a popular beach on a sunny day. Indistinct voices chattered happily above the sounds of sea birds and crashing waves. Music played in the background, growing louder and fainter as unseen traffic passed. It zoomed in on a trio of young women walking past in skimpy bikinis, bronze bodies on full display. After a few moments, the view widened in search of other interesting sights.

Of the hundreds of beachgoers in frame, lying on towels, playing pickle ball or frisbee, standing in the surf, or playing in the sand, a red circle formed around one middle-aged man walking onto frame. His thong looked homemade, from palm fronds or something, and he must have really been into tanning. He was Bronze bronze. The only other things he wore were a bead necklace and a funky ear expander. He was either a total hipster or a native.

"Dude, why are you showing me this?" James asked.

"Just watch." I pointed out the man as if the red circle wasn't enough.

He remained on the edge of the frame. The person filming was more interested in a couple women nearby with dripping ice cream cones.

The man just stood there, smiling, looking out

155

toward the sea. Then he bent over backward, and boom.

The man vanished, and the people around him were covered in red. A gray cloud followed a moment later, as did the screams. The view jiggled, but remained on the subject a moment longer while the apparent shock wore off. People started running in all directions, emerging from the cloud covered in what looked like ash. Yelling in a foreign language, and the view panned chaotically as the cameraman ran.

Legs, cars, street, trash, neon signs all came into view and vanished as quickly. Perhaps thirty seconds later, the view steadied and turned back toward the beach. It was deserted now, save for a woman dragging her child from the surf by one arm, but the view zoomed in to a section of sand, stained red. In the center stood a bone-white pillar that hadn't been there before.

"Look familiar?" I asked.

"That's fake," he said. I raised an eyebrow. "Come on, it's clearly fake. Someone posted it after seeing the nightclub footage, just trying to get views."

"Okay, this is a post of a post of a post, because they keep taking them down, but the original was supposed to be from four days before The Woods."

"A post of a post of a post? Do you even hear yourself? That's total urban legend stuff. If something like this happened, why wasn't it filmed by a hundred different people? Why didn't we hear about it a week ago?"

"I don't know. Maybe they did, but this is the one

that went viral. Here's the thing that gets me, though. That's Copacabana beach, in Rio De Janeiro. The girl from The Woods still hasn't been identified. How many people do you suppose knew she was from Rio? And she said she was sick all week. She could have been on that beach before leaving for New York."

"Did you see her?"

"What?"

"In the video. Did you find her? Point her out to me, and I'll believe you."

"It's shaky-cam, man! And the cameraman was drooling over asses. I couldn't make out a single face except for the ice cream girls."

"I don't know what to tell you then, Willy. It looks fake to me."

"You know I hate when you call me that. How are you feeling?"

He gave me an odd look, like I was calling him out. Blaming him or something. "I don't feel like exploding, if that's what you mean."

"Be serious. You're sick. You're sleeping way too much, and I heard you coughing all night. Sounding like Isaac Hayes with a head cold, and this stiffness is worrying me."

"I'm not sick. I just don't feel so good. Watching someone explode will do that to you."

"Watching someone explode doesn't screw up your throat."

"Yeah, but smoke inhalation does, and I got that full in the face too, thank you very much."

"The CDC was here a bit ago. The cops too. They showed me your picture and asked if I knew you."

James sat up straight, his eyes going wide. "What did you say?"

"I lied to them, obviously, or they'd be talking to you instead of me. But I'm starting to think I shouldn't have."

"Dude, screw this stupid video, and how it's framing the narrative! What happened at The Woods was a terrorist event. Some bastard put a bomb on that poor girl, and acting like this is some communicable disease is belittling that. Someone needs to be held accountable. That's why the cops were here. They blame me. Or they want to. Anyone they can say for sure was there, just to make the story go away. And meanwhile, Hezbollah, or the Colombians, or hell, Russia, are laughing their asses off."

I was silent for a while. It was hard to argue in the face of such passion. It always had been. "Maybe," I finally said. "But if you're still feeling like crap tomorrow, I'm taking you to see a doctor."

His face twisted in anger, and he filled his lungs to respond, but I cut him off.

"We don't have to mention The Woods. You can keep the three-days-growth of beard, and maybe part your hair different. Since you aren't covered in blood, no one's going to recognize you. We'll just get you checked out."

He deflated. "We'll see. Right now, I reek. I'm going to take a shower while you order lunch. Do you got Jimmy John's out here?"

"Yeah." I chuckled. Jimmy from the sticks asking if we've got stuff in New York.

"Good. I would murder for a number twelve right now."

* * *

He was more active that afternoon, but had zero interest in talking about what happened any further. Instead, we binge-watched stuff he'd missed while at college. He went to bed early, and that was it.

The next morning, the old James was back.

I can't tell you how relieved I was. His voice was still a little smokey, but at least it didn't sound like he had a wood chipper for vocal cords.

"How'd you sleep?" I asked as soon as he emerged.

"Great. I've actually been up for hours. I just wanted to make sure I gave you time to sleep."

"Me?" I smiled.

"Yeah. I know I've been a bit of a downer, and you've been all worried. Probably kept you up. But I'm going to make up for that."

I narrowed my eyes, but got off the couch and set the blankets aside. "What do you have up your sleeve?" I asked.

"Oh, I've got plans, alright. The Yankees are playing a day game, and I switched my flight for a red-eye. I got us seats on the third base line. First tier."

"You *have* been busy. How'd you score that?" I

didn't particularly care to watch organized sports, but I was getting into it, just seeing James excited.

He shrugged. "Some scalper site. Cost me an arm and a leg, but who cares? I'm in New York, and I'm going to a Yankees game." He flashed me the broadest smile I've seen in ages.

But I couldn't help thinking of the James who went to bed early the night before. At risk of dumping ashes on the mood, I asked, "Are you sure you're up for that?"

"Dude, I feel so good. I can't even tell you. It's my last day, and I've wasted the previous two. Let's just be brothers and go see a game."

I put my hands up. "Okay. You've got me. I'm in."

It was my turn to wash the last few days off of me, and when I came out of the shower, James was stretched out on the couch with Salsa music playing on the Alexa, and another glass of the ill-advised tap water in his hand. Before I could say anything, he took a drink.

I made a face, but he smacked his lips. "God, it's amazing."

"What is?"

"That feeling, after you've been sick, you know, and you can breathe again? And the air just smells so sweet?" He looked at the glass in his hand. "It's like, you never notice how good water tastes. It's just water. You drink it because you're thirsty. But after you've been feeling bad, it's the most amazing thing. Nothing added to it, no particular flavor, but it just

160

tastes. So. Good." He smiled up at me in that infectious way. You just want to laugh.

I smiled back. "Come on. We'll take the subway."

We'd dodged a bullet. With all the talk of anthrax, and the CDC not knowing what it was, and that video from Rio... I'd been sure James was going to die. But he was back, and even more so.

I couldn't remember the last time I'd seen him so happy. My worries melted, and I saw the world through his eyes. The subway wasn't a commute. It was an event. The people on it all had stories and lives, and they were fascinating.

We bought souvenir flags and overpriced beer, and hot, fresh peanuts. Then yelled at the other team's batters, and we mocked the umpires for questionable calls. We sang the songs they broadcast, we played the games they threw up during inning changes, and we laughed.

It was probably the most fun I'd had since moving to the city.

"Hey, man," James said, putting a hand on my knee. "I'm going to go drain the lizard. Don't score any runs while I'm gone, okay?"

I laughed, and so did he, and he got up and squeezed past our neighbors to the aisle.

He took another look back at me, still smiling, then started up the steep stairs. His foot missed the first one. A look of confusion came over his face, and he stopped.

Dread seized hold of me. It was like waking from a dream. His mood, our happy times, the entire morning popped like a bubble, and he was just another Brazilian girl dancing in a nightclub.

I stood up, but I couldn't speak. The blood drained from my body, and my limbs went weak.

A smile flashed across James's face, but the confusion was back a moment later. Then his face twisted and stretched. His eyes rolled back, and he gripped the central hand rail like he was magnetically attached.

Slowly, his body bent backward, nearly double. This, finally, got the attention of everyone around him. The crowd, at least those within a dozen seats of him, went silent. Some of them stood. Everyone held their breath.

"No," I croaked.

Boom.

James disappeared faster than I could see, and I was pelted with tiny objects, like sand. Something hit my eyeball, and I squeezed them shut, turning my face away. Shards of bone and blobs of goo hit the back of my head.

People screamed.

I screamed.

I opened my eyes to see everyone around covered in gore. The day had gone dark. The sun filtered through a layer of haze hanging over the stands. Someone in the row behind me stood, nearly knocking me over. I reached for the back of the seat in front of me, then I was hit from behind and I went down.

People were running, screaming. I got hit repeatedly. Stepped on. My head banged against the concrete and I raised it again and again, trying to stand. I managed to get on all fours when the coughing fit hit and I couldn't rise any further. Someone stepped on my hand. My fingers rolled, bones crunched. I screamed in pain.

The stampede died down, and I stood, cradling my fingers in my armpit. What had started here had expanded, and the entire stadium was emptying, leaving trampled bodies among empty seats. Even the field had cleared.

I was alone with the pillar that stood in place of my brother.

It was rooted to the concrete stairs—no, not rooted so much as melted into it, like epoxy poured over the surface and bonding with it. And that tall, bone white termite mound of a pillar jutted up from it. Steam wafted off the surface.

I had the urge to touch it. It reminded me of stalagmites I'd seen in a Tennessee cavern when I was a kid. Smooth, but pockmarked with holes. Organic, but alien. The surrounding area was soaked in blood and covered in dust, but the pillar stood pristine. I snapped a picture of it.

My fingers sizzled on contact with it. I drew back from the rock-hard surface. Of course. That kind of rapid reaction would produce a lot of heat.

But this was all that was left of my brother. His monument. His grave marker. I felt tied to it, but it seemed like I should feel more. Was this shock? My brother was dead. Where was the grief? The pain? I plumbed my feelings.

I found fear.

Worse than fear, it was terror. People were coming for me. James had been right. The government, the police, anyone in a position of power, was going to want to explain this event, and they would pin the blame on me.

Everyone else had run. They would catch me, the last one there. I had to go, get lost in the crowd until I found somewhere safe.

I can't tell you what the next hour was like. I only remember flashes. I'm pretty sure I did some trampling of my own getting out of the stadium, and I vividly remember punching someone who got between me and a closing subway door. A cop? Maybe. I only remember her eyes and the sound of her skull bouncing off the tiles.

All I know is I made it home. Even that didn't feel safe. The cops had been there already. They knew where I lived, but I had no place else to go. I closed the blinds again, reminded of James's need for darkness. Whatever he had, I bloody well had it now.

I did what I always did when something scared me. I researched. Somehow, knowing everything about something always made it less frightening.

I locked myself in the bathroom, climbed into the tub with my laptop. The pain in my hands drew attention away from my purpose and I examined them by the light of my screen. My fingertips on one hand were seared smooth.

The three middle fingers of my other hand were stiff and going black. They throbbed painfully. They needed medical attention, but the certainty that they would lock me up and vivisect me for the other thing kept me from seeking help.

I uploaded the picture from my phone. It nagged at me how I'd seen something like it before. While I've been calling it a pillar, it had none of the symmetry of one, and even the comparison to stalagmites was not quite right. I ran an image search to see what it reminded Google's algorithm of.

Pictures of stalagmites came up, as did termite mounds, but also mushrooms, tons of them. Videos as well, time lapsed videos of mushrooms blooming and launching their spores into the wind. That gave me a chill, looking quite a bit like the gray cloud that followed all three explosions I'd seen. It still wasn't quite right.

The next picture showed a dead ant with a white pillar sticking out of its head. That was it, the exact thing. The caption read Ophiocordyceps unilateralis. I copied that and pasted it into another search tab.

It was a parasitic fungus specific to carpenter ants, but there were over four hundred related species that specialized in everything from other ants to moths, grasshoppers to wasps, and even frogs.

Each version was specific to one animal, but the process was the same for each. The animal got infected, its behavior immediately changed to better suit the fungus's growth, then it reached maturity, and the animal sought out a location where it could infect the most of its kind. Then, in an instant, the fungus grew a "fruiting body" out through its victim, killing it instantly.

The interesting thing about the ants was that they knew about this fungus. Guard ants recognized the infected, carried them far from the colony, and killed them. In response to that, the fungus-zombies stopped trying to enter the colony, instead hanging from a leaf above it. Far enough away not to be noticed, but close enough to infect a thousand others.

Thinking back to the Rio video, I wondered if that man on the beach came from the same area of the jungle where these ants lived.

I left the bathroom and turned on the news. It was a while before they mentioned Yankee Stadium, because at right about the same time, two people exploded at opposite ends of Coney Island, and another in a tour group of the Capitol building in Washington, D.C.

Since then, others have gone off across the western hemisphere, in major cities and public places. All at right about two PM, local time. Sporting events, concerts and festivals, one state fair, a couple of shopping malls, the beach at Cancun, and a Costco in the Midwest.

America was in lockdown. Citizens were ordered to remain in their homes, and anyone who was exposed to one of these attackers was to identify themselves. A special hotline had been set up. The CDC had isolated an unknown fungal spore from the attack at The Woods, and pharmaceutical companies were ramping up production of anti-fungal medications.

People were told to monitor family members for uncharacteristic behavior, and isolate anyone who was acting paranoid or overly enthusiastic, then call the hotline.

I switched the television off.

If this was altering human behavior like it did in ants, I was going to do the opposite of what I felt like. Fungus grows best in the dark, so I crossed the room to the blinds and grabbed the cord.

Fear gripped me. I didn't know who was out there, who might be watching. Were people already turning in their family members? Wasn't it paranoia to imagine that your family has changed behavior? By definition, the ones who were turning people in should themselves be taken into custody.

And what were they doing with the people they picked up? Were we to trust the government? Would these anti-fungals even work?

I steeled myself and opened the blinds. The setting sun streamed in, stabbing my eyeballs with searing hot pain. I crumpled under the weight of it, screwing my eyes shut and nearly vomiting from pain and nausea. Slowly, I steadied my breathing, got a hold of myself.

It was dark here, beneath the windowsill, but the red glow of late-day sun reflected painfully off the TV screen. I wanted to stand, to defy this feeling and bask in the sun's fading rays like a vampire tired of life, but pain was an excellent teacher.

Besides, I remembered there was a security camera on the shop at the end of the block, and I'm pretty sure it had a good view of my window. By now, the government was probably tapping those, doing facial recognition on anyone who was at the stadium.

I spent the next couple of days hiding from the outside world, drinking tons of water and watching videos of how much worse it was getting out there.

The chaos hadn't ended in the Americas. At two PM in Tokyo, Osaka, and Kyoto, office buildings and train stations emptied as panicked citizens fled similar explosions. China tried to get ahead of things and ordered everyone home, but that sent the streets of all their major cities into gridlock when people started exploding and the chaos couldn't be contained.

Moscow was just waking up when this happened, and locked the country down, too late for the eastern reaches, but hopefully limiting exposure in their more populated regions. Unfortunately, most Russians lived in colossal apartment blocks that shared a single ventilation system, and clouds of dust billowed out of every vent.

Saudi Arabia, Turkey, Israel all tried similar methods with varying degrees of success. Major cities across Europe and Africa pleaded with their populations to stay at home, but by then, large protests were forming over government inaction, ineffective mandates, and increasing reports of military injustices.

My phone buzzed, reading Centers for Disease

Control. As soon as I saw it, I locked myself in the bathroom again. They were probably demanding that I come in. But it occurred to me, the longer I went without responding, the more likely I would have cops knocking down my door.

Eventually, I crept out and picked up my phone. It was only a text message informing me that my blood work was clean. I almost laughed at the absurdity. They clearly didn't know I was at the ball game. But a second thought choked the laughter off in my throat. Maybe they knew, and they sent the message to catch me off guard when they knocked on my door in.

I turned off my phone and ripped out the sim card in case they were tracking it. I wanted to get somewhere else, somewhere they wouldn't find me, but where? I didn't have any cash on me, and if I used my credit card to get a hotel room, they could trace that.

Back home, to the Midwest. My folks would take me in. But how would I get there? I didn't have a car, and renting one or taking a train would mean using my card again. Could I steal a car? I had neither the skill to hot wire one, nor a weapon to carjack someone with. Unless I counted my dull-bladed old Leatherman.

So, I locked myself in the bathroom and sat in the tub, too scared to open my laptop in case they tracked my IP address. To satisfy my desperate thirst and soothe this aching throat, I drank straight from the tap. It tasted horrible, but it was better than leaving the safety of my dark space.

But this morning, I realized the government didn't

have the resources for everything that worried me. Besides, I knew I was going to die soon. I'd come to terms with that. I'd had a good life, and looking back at all the laughter and loving friends, I was ready to go.

The pain in my joints was gone, and it didn't hurt to swallow. Even my blackened fingers didn't hurt anymore, though they smelled funky as hell. It was time to stop hiding and go out into the world again.

There were just two things I wanted to do before I died. Number one was to finish this journal, because I feel confident that a cure is right around the corner, and this may be the key to finding it. After that, I've always wanted to see the view from the top of the Empire State Building.

Just one more drink from the tap first, because, damn, it tastes so good.

Ichabod Ebenezer is the genre-promiscuous author of *A Shadow Stained in Blood* and the horror short story collection, *Beyond the Rail and Other Nightmares*. He lives and writes in the Pacific Northwest with his family, a chameleon, and the ghosts of three cats. He is currently pitching a Dark Fantasy novel.

About the Authors

Dear Authors of The Start,
We are nothing without you.
Love, Rebellion LIT

As our first contributors, the talented authors featured in The Start proved to be brilliant, daring, and rebellious.

If you loved a story, and you want more info about the author, links to additional reads, and social media, please visit https://rebellionlit.com/authors-of-the-start/ to learn more.

Be sure to mention your favorite stories in your review.

Also From Rebellion LIT

Kisses in the Dark by Marlowe Westley Pulliam

Elevated Inferno by Carlotta Ardell

Helpless: A short story collection by Tiffany Christina Lewis

Alyssa Fairfield by Tiffany Christina Lewis

The Michael Taylor Series